THE REASON YOU'RE ALIVE

ALSO BY MATTHEW QUICK

Every Exquisite Thing

Love May Fail

The Good Luck of Right Now

Forgive Me, Leonard Peacock

Boy21

Sorta Like a Rock Star

The Silver Linings Playbook

THE REASON YOU'RE ALIVE

A NOVEL

MATTHEW QUICK

HARPER AVENUE

This is a work of fiction. Names, characters, places, and incidents are products of the author's imagination or are used fictitiously and are not to be construed as real. Any resemblance to actual events, locales, organizations, or persons, living or dead, is entirely coincidental.

Published by Harper Avenue, an imprint of
HarperCollins Publishers Ltd

First Canadian edition

HarperCollins Publishers Ltd
2 Bloor Street East, 20th Floor
Toronto, Ontario, Canada
M4W 1A8

Designed by Leah Carlson-Stanisic

www.harpercollins.ca

Library and Archives Canada Cataloguing in Publication
information is available upon request.

ISBN 978-1-44345-345-5 (hardcover)
ISBN 978-1-44344-809-3 (original trade paperback)

Printed and bound in the United States
LSC/H 9 8 7 6 5 4 3 2 1

FOR UNCLE PETE

THE REASON YOU'RE ALIVE

1.

The doctors were giving me the mushroom treatment—keeping me in the dark and feeding me bullshit.

I didn't call them on the subterfuge because I just wanted out of the hospital ASAP, and that required making the people in charge think I was docile. I knew without a doubt that your current employer was still keeping tabs on me, almost five decades after my discharge.

"Who is Clayton Fire Bear?" the doctors kept asking, only they used his real name, because I apparently kept saying it over and over when I first woke up postoperation. To protect the innocent, Clayton Fire Bear is the fake name I'll be using in this report. I'm not gonna tell you his real name. I also wasn't about to tell those civilian morons at the hospital what I'm finally telling you right here and now.

Doctors are only ever one of three things: pill pushers, needle pokers, or people cutters. All of them love money. Needless to say, they get paid regardless of what messes they make of our bodies. Even if they kill us dead, the doctors' paychecks remain healthy, and their bank accounts grow.

The people cutter in charge of my brain surgery shit show

said I absorbed a twin when I was in my late mother's womb, back in 1944, which would make me a murderer before I was even born. You people would *love* for that to be true, because it would take the United States government off the hook for teaching me how.

My dumbass neurosurgeon said part of that aforementioned alleged twin grew in my brain for almost seventy years, and the mass they removed from my skull had hair and three tiny teeth that looked like uncooked grains of rice. I was shown a specimen in a bottle of formaldehyde as proof, but you and I and everyone else with a working brain know they had a million and one of those exhibits before I even walked into the hospital, so that little bottle doesn't prove shit. Furthermore, he said my condition was so rare, he was gonna write a story on what he calls "our surgery" and get paid again, and why wouldn't he?

If you believe that absorbed-twin horseshit, you deserve the dumb life you're currently living. I know it was Agent Orange. The cover-up continues.

I'm also one hundred percent certain that, at the request of the US government, my surgeon chopped out some of my memory when they were inside my skull, erasing the vital military intelligence I once possessed and even personal memories too, about my wife and my presurgery life, just to be sadistic. But no matter how many chemicals they spray on you, no matter how much of your memory they slice away, you never forget seeing an entire jungle disappear overnight. One day everything's full and green and lush and breathing. The next day everything's melted thin and black and stagnant—as if the world were a candle and the sun were a blowtorch. I remember death's stench darting up my nostrils like an ice pick. You can *never* unexperience that. Never get entirely free of that chemical decay smell either.

I have a visible souvenir too: seven little white spots on my left forearm. The doctors say it's simply damage from the sun, but they don't know shit, or else you people—aka the government—have paid them to lie. Seven drops of Agent Orange hit my left forearm when I was in the jungle. I've been wearing the unlucky constellation ever since.

My son says if you connect the white dots with your mind, it looks like a map of Vietnam, but that's bullshit too. Hank may be a hotshot art dealer now, but he still doesn't know goddamn anything about my war or my life.

I'm surprised you people didn't pay my surgeon to saw off my entire fucking arm when they had me knocked out—just to get rid of all remaining evidence that incriminates your traitorous boss, Uncle Sam.

But, ironically, at the end of this report, you'll see I was most grateful that your surgeon's scalpel tickled my memories of Clayton Fire Bear—that big motherfucking Indian—and got me thinking about righting my wrongs.

But I can't tell you everything about Fire Bear before I put it all in context. I want you to understand, and understanding is difficult. Takes time. Patience. Which I hope you will really have, like you've assured me so many times already.

The aforementioned girly-man surgeon has never even fired a gun. I asked him. His nose wrinkled in disgust. I told him the great jihad was on, and that the Muslim suicide bombers would just keep coming if we don't do something serious about it, and quickly, but he didn't care enough about that to respond. Too much people-cutting to do. Too much money to make. Too much high living in the land of the free.

When I pushed the issue with the people cutter, referencing the two scumbags who blew up the Boston Marathon, my surgeon said he didn't want to speak about politics. And why would he, really? He's on top here at the hospital. Big dog. Things are working out just fine for him right now. He probably has no family in the military, no blood on the ground in Iraq or Afghanistan. My surgeon still has all his limbs and all his easy happy civilian memories. No thick red scar stapled shut on top of his head. No little white dots on his forearm either. No recurring nightmares for fifty fucking years. No daily horror show playing inside his skull.

I obviously needed to buddy up with the guy, so he'd eventually release me once again to walk among the civilians. So I asked him what he liked to do for fun when he's not working, and without making eye contact, he said he enjoyed "quaffing fine wines."

Dead end.

I was a beer guy before all the brain troubles. American beer. Budweiser. Miller High Life. PBR. With the medication I was already on—a fucking arm's length of orange pill bottles full of shit I can't even pronounce—my drinking days were done. Turns out I liked breathing more than brewskies.

I know what *quaffing* means, but I'd never use that word. Makes you sound like an elitist asshole. You can tell a lot about a man by the alcohol he drinks. "Quaffing fine wines" meant we were at an impasse.

You can also judge the strength of a man's character by the condition of his hands. My surgeon's hands look like they're made of the smoothest china. He wouldn't have lasted ten seconds in the jungle. I might have put a bullet in the back of his head myself as a safety precaution. You don't get out of the jungle alive with men who "quaff fine wines."

"Try not to think about upsetting things like politics and war," my surgeon said to me. "Happy thoughts are your brain's vitamins, so try to think happy thoughts with each breath in and happy thoughts with each breath out, okay?"

He balanced on one foot, closed his eyes, put his left ankle on his right knee, and—pressing his hands together in front of his heart—he did some deep-breathing yoga bullshit. Then he said, "Can you do this for me, Mr. Granger?"

I could not, and I told him I couldn't even stand yet, let alone perform some stork posture like a goddamn ballerina in a little pink tutu.

And respected medical professionals say this deep-breathing surgeon is one of the best in the entire world.

"Who is Clayton Fire Bear?" he asked me once more, with a glint in his eye that suggested he knew I had a big secret.

Men like him don't deserve to know my secrets. I didn't tell the people cutter any of what follows.

2.

My mostly ignorant son, Hank, dropped by my hospital room just to scream at me.

Doctors had sawed through my skull. They had cut out part of my brain. I was still freeballing it in a lime-green fairy gown. I was in a fucking hospital bed, for Christ's sake, and Hank's machine-gunning me with entire belts of words just because I didn't tell him about the surgery until after it was over. I figured, why worry him? We hadn't been speaking since summer anyway. Ever since we had a blowout at the Phillies game.

Me, Hank, and my granddaughter, Ella, were waiting in line for hot dogs. We hadn't yet eaten dinner because my son had worked late again, picking us up well into the second inning, and so we didn't even enter Citizens Bank Park until the bottom of the fourth, by which time Ella and I were ready to start eating our own hands. The line was long. Hank had something up his ass, and even Ella felt the fuck-yous coming through his skin like sweat. I knew, because she kept grabbing my hand and squeezing it. Any idiot could tell that she was nervous.

When we got to the front of the line, the cashier was wearing one of those scary—and sexist by anyone's standards, but will my liberal son ever say that? Hell, no!—black headdresses that cover everything but the eyes. And in ninety-degree heat, no less. Her sweat was seeping through the fabric.

That headdress looked like a torture device. If a conservative Republican candidate said women should cover their faces in public, he'd be assassinated by feminazis before the sun set. But those same liberals who hate conservative Christians will protect Muslim rights.

What were they hiding under those black tents they made their women wear?

I didn't want to know.

So I did the classiest thing this American patriot could think of—I shook my head, put my unwrapped hot dog down on the counter, and walked away in protest. No woman should be forced to cover her face in public. That's bullshit. Un-American.

The poor brainwashed Muslim lady started yelling at me through the black fabric, saying, "You never heard of the First Amendment? Freedom of religion?"

I had fought for those things. Watched my buddies die so that she was free to wear that fucking Muslim torture device in my country. So I was damn well entitled to my opinion. She could wear it, but that didn't mean I had to buy food from her. Freedom goes both ways.

As I walked away, I heard Hank making a big production of apologizing on my behalf and then paying for the hot dogs—no doubt leaving a massive guilt-based tip, "acknowledging his privilege," whatever the fuck that means—and then he came after me, dragging Ella by the arm. His face was the color of a ripe Jersey tomato. Hers was white as fresh milk.

He started screaming at me in front of a growing crowd of strangers in red Phillies caps that matched ours, saying I was an embarrassment and that if I couldn't "put a lid on" my "racism" he was gonna ban me from seeing Ella, who at this point was staring hard at her fancy sneakers that actually lit up when she walked.

Lights in sneakers. Now that's some spoiled rich-girl shit, right?

But I like Ella, and she likes me. Her parents hadn't fucked her up too much, which was a bit of a miracle.

I asked Hank how my walking away made me a racist when the Muslim veil had prevented me from even seeing what race the woman was, which is when he switched to calling me a bigot, conceding the point.

I told him he had better learn to know his enemy, because the great jihad was on and there's a reason the Jews don't let "peaceful, nonviolent" Germans wear swastikas in Israel—and that's when Hank marched Ella and me out of the stadium and drove us home in silence.

We never even went to our seats, which were right behind home plate. Kendrick was on the mound. One of Hank's big-shot clients had provided the tickets for free. And yet we didn't even see a single pitch. What a fucking waste. And all because the Muslims had invaded our national pastime.

When Hank dropped me off, he said, "We will not speak to

you again until you apologize for your abhorrent vile behavior. It's 2013!"

"Fine," I said, and got out of the car.

As he drove away, I saw Ella's sad eyes looking out through the back window, and I thought, She's doomed without me.

Hank's wife, Femke—yes, that is her real name, pronounced *Fem*-kah—no doubt took his side and fueled the fuck-your-apelike-father fire. Femke calls me Aap—pronounced *ahhh*-p—because that means "ape" in Dutch, her native tongue. Fuck her.

Either way, months passed without a word from him, which I didn't mind so much. But I missed Ella terribly. I thought about trying to break her out of school for a few hours, saying she needed to visit the dentist, but I knew my she-devil daughter-in-law would have me arrested, and I didn't want to put Ella in a position where she'd have to lie to her parents, because the guilt would have eaten her up.

She's a great kid, Ella. I'm telling you. The spitting image of her American grandmother—my dead wife, Jessica.

I'm a dangerous right-wing grandpa. And I own guns too. Lots of them. Some registered, some we don't talk about. I'm an education full of truth and experience that contradicts the never-ending bullshit Professor Femke Turk teaches young people at her "sister school" university.

My daughter-in-law's parents emigrated from the Netherlands when she was a teenager, so she has "European sensibilities," which is code for even fucking dumber than regular US liberals. She didn't take our family name, that's how much she hates me. And to make matters even worse, my granddaughter's official name is hyphenated: Ella Turk-Granger. I thought only Mexicans hyphenated names, but apparently the Dutch do too. At least the one I know does. My son didn't have the stones to put a stop to that, which broke my father's heart.

So I don't think Hank and my Phillies-game disagreement was really about Jihad Jenny selling swine hot dogs and American beer—the consumption of which the Muslim religion forbids, which makes her a hypocrite anyway. The Taliban would stone her to death and cut off her head for a trophy, which is why she prefers America, and don't you forget it.

When my brain got all fucked up and I crashed my BMW and the doctors told me I needed to go under the knife, I kept the medical report to myself. I knew I wasn't gonna die. Only the good die young, and I had lived nasty. I've done things you can't even imagine.

The postsurgery problem was this: the doctors wouldn't release me from the hospital unless I was accompanied, and I didn't want to put that on any of my good friends, hence the call to my only son. To be one hundred percent honest, one of my best friends ultimately pressured me into making that call when she finally figured out I hadn't let my son know I was in the hospital, but I'm gonna talk about Sue—who just so happens to be genetically Vietnamese—later and not now.

"You can't live on your own anymore," Hank said in my hospital room.

"The fuck I can't!" I said, holding onto my dog tags, which were rubber-banded together with my father's and hung around my neck for good luck. I told my son it wasn't my time to kick the bucket. I wasn't buying the bullet just yet, so he was gonna have to deal with me for a little while longer. "Sorry for the inconvenience."

He kept saying, "What are we going to do with you?" like I wasn't even there.

I told him he could just drop me off at home. If he was feeling kind, he could get me a cheesesteak from Donkey's Place in Camden, which he never would have done, because it's in a rough black neighborhood. Despite being so-called liberals, my son and his wife don't mix much with black people, especially blacks without at least two fancy degrees.

Me, I've always got along with the brothers. I have no problems with them. Always tried to get them jobs whenever I could because it used to be hard for blacks to find steady employment here in America. They have been here a long time. Fought wars with us. Survived slavery even. You have to be a tough motherfucking race to survive slavery. I tip my hat to the Jews here too. But they got their own country already, and Egypt was a hell of a long time ago. Blacks deserve more than recent modern immigrants who want to take over the country five seconds after they arrive, but try saying that to the likes of Hank and Femke. I even like legal Mexicans too, because they are hardworking. I always hire legal Mexicans to do my lawn work. You'd be a fool to hire a white man.

The hospital food was inedible. Fucking Jell-O is not a meal. The snakes I killed and cooked in Vietnam just to stay alive tasted better than the shit they served there. They charge a small fortune for it too, whether you eat it or not. Robbery. I tell you. Might as well have held a gun to my head and taken my wallet while I was too sick to get out of bed. Bastards. They should shoot all hospital executives, along with every single politician.

"So you admit you can't get out of bed," my son said triumphantly, like he had caught me in a lie.

So I told him, *at first*, I couldn't get out of bed. They chiseled and sawed my fucking skull open, for Christ's sake. I wasn't the goddamn man of steel. I admitted it. But I'd since recovered. And I had been able to get out of bed for days. Took a week and a bucket of stool softeners just to get me shitting again. But I made that happen too.

He didn't think I could walk, so I gave him a demonstration by taking a leak in the attached bathroom. When I returned, Hank looked at me like I was Jesus Fucking Christ walking around with holes through my wrists and ankles, but the expression on his face wasn't a happy one, which was when I realized he was rooting for me to be put away somewhere or simply die.

He said I needed to be monitored, and I said he was dead wrong, which was when he started crying about looking bad in front of the doctors and nurses, saying they had given him quite a guilt trip for not coming earlier. Apparently, he felt he had to explain to the entire fucking world the reasons that he and I weren't speaking, which he said wasn't "a fun conversation" for him.

"And who is this Clayton Fire Bear?" he asked.

Hank didn't deserve to know the answer to that particular

question just yet. Instead, I told him that doctors and nurses are paid good money, so you don't have to explain shit to them, but he just kept crying about what the hospital staff thought of him as if they thought anything at all. Did he not realize that we're all just meat, and that slabs of meat are run in and out of hospitals around the clock every day of the year?

Hank raked his fingers through the little hair he has left on top. He should have shaved his head ten years ago, but that would make him look like his army vet father, and his European wife wouldn't want that. She'd rather have everyone talk behind Hank's back, laughing the whole time at the few long strands of hair he's clinging to.

Then Hank said, "What if you had died in surgery and we never got to say good-bye?"

There were girly-man tears in his eyes, and he was blinking more than a sweet little actress trying to win a golden trophy. No doubt he was thinking about his mother again.

"I'll know when I'm gonna die," I told him. "Everyone who survived the Vietnam jungle is well acquainted with Death. I know that motherfucker better than you know yourself."

"This isn't time for your superstitions," my son said, because he didn't know goddamn anything.

His biggest opponents in life were the foreign she-devil he *chose* to sleep with and the heart-attack-inducing civilian stress he created for himself. Hank's never really had to confront anything too challenging. Like most Americans today, he had been afforded the luxury of naïveté. His life had never been on the line. He never had to wipe his face clean of his friends' blood and guts. Never had a Vietnamese anatomy lesson. Never tried to scoop up his buddy's steaming hot insides off the jungle floor and make them into a person again.

You'd think he'd thank veterans like me for that gift of naïveté, but you'd be wrong. Not even on November 11. Instead, he voted *against* a man who actually survived the Hanoi Hilton. The boy I raised from birth campaigned and voted for a man named Barack Hussein Obama. Hank celebrated like he had single-handedly won a war when the liberals took over the White House. McCain never had a prayer.

3.

It's hard to talk about war with people who haven't seen real action. You don't understand. You will *never* understand. And so I can't tell you everything. But if you listen the right way, you might just learn a thing or two anyway.

My father served in World War II under Patton. Stormed Normandy. When I was little, I used to ask him about his war experience, hoping for epic stories full of gunfire, tanks, and Nazi-killing glory. When I was a kid, he only ever told me two tales. Neither had anything to do with death or violence.

The first was about stumbling onto an abandoned champagne warehouse outside Paris after Europe had been liberated. He and his buddies were given an hour to drink their fill, and so they did, spraying each other with endless bottles of France's finest bubbles, "more than the average American could buy with an entire year's salary."

The second story my father told me was about his being run over by a US jeep in the middle of the night. He was too tired to dig his foxhole deep enough, and consequently a jeep ran over his leg while he was sleeping, fracturing his shinbone. He was sent to Paris to recover.

According to the story, he would sneak out of the hospital at night on crutches, find the nearest bar, and try to pass himself off as a famous American singer, not yet big in Europe. The next Frank Sinatra, or something like that.

"After the war ends, you'll be hearing my name everywhere," he lied.

The French enjoyed his singing so much, a local artist painted my father's likeness onto the wall of a big Parisian club, or so the legend goes.

I was maybe ten when I found a German officer's uniform in our attic—swastika armband and all. There were two bullet holes through the chest and two ruby-black bull's-eyes of dried blood. Even back then I realized there was only one way you acquired such an artifact. When I asked my father about it, I was wearing the SS Nazi officer hat. On the front of it, an eagle perched on a swastika with its wings spread wide. Underneath that was a skull and crossbones. When I was a kid, I didn't know any better, so I just put it on my head. I thought it looked pretty badass, which was the fucking point, I guess. Hitler Youth. That Führer knew how to recruit, let me tell you.

Understandably, in hindsight now, my old man went from calm to wild-eyed in point-five seconds and began striking me on the side of the head with an open hand. The first pop caught me square on the ear, which produced a loud ringing and sent that Nazi cap flying across the room. My old man never hit me with a closed fist, and I never hit Hank with a closed fist either. Not once.

Outside, my father threw the whole Nazi uniform into an empty oil drum we kept in the backyard for burning trash. He poured a gallon of gasoline on top. But when he lit the match, he hesitated, and it burned itself out between his finger and thumb. He kept lighting matches, but he wouldn't drop them in. I was watching through my bedroom window. After seven or so matches went out, he finally remembered he had Nazi-killing stones between his thighs and did the deed. I could see his entire body shaking from fifty yards away, silhouetted by the rising flames.

I didn't fully understand what I had seen until a decade later, when I caught a Vietnamese peasant smearing chicken blood on VC uniforms, back in the jungle. We all knew this guy and used him often to get information only connected locals would know. These people were so poor any one of them would bring you his own mother's head for a hundred US dollars. That was like ten million dollars to them.

We nicknamed this guy Ding-Dong because he would just appear out of thin air, and when we saw him, someone would always yell, "Ding-Dong!" which he liked to repeat with a huge grin on his face.

In the jungle many of us collected Vietnamese souvenirs. I collected weapons, taking knives and guns off dead gooks. Other guys collected ears or trigger fingers.

That Indian motherfucker who absolutely hated my guts and swore to kill me—as I said, I'll talk later about Clayton Fire Bear, whose name I have changed to protect the innocent—used to scalp the Vietcong and wear those scalps on his belt. He had enough so that it looked like a foul miniskirt of hair.

But there were uniform collectors too. Some US military

guys—like priests and mechanics and cooks and some medics—were lucky enough to never leave the base, and therefore never got to kill the enemy. But they wanted their souvenirs too, so they often bought them from Ding-Dong. Only they thought they were buying the real deal, that he had stripped uniforms off dead VC. So when I caught him smearing chicken blood on fake uniforms, I knew I had him. If I told the men to whom he had sold memorabilia, men who had paid good money for VC blood, they would have slit his throat without blinking, and Ding-Dong knew it. We locked eyes in the jungle, and I didn't have to say I owned him. Every cell in his yellow body knew it.

I nodded.

He nodded back.

And the pact was sworn.

I'd call in that favor a little later on during my tour.

But that's how I came to understand my father's violent reaction to my finding that Nazi uniform in the attic, and the way he shook as he watched it burn in the old oil drum.

My old man didn't pay a Ding-Dong for his Nazi uniform. He did his killing fair and square and stripped his own dead. He couldn't tell me that when I was a boy. There was no way to explain to a civilian—let alone a child—why he needed to bring that bloody Nazi uniform back across the Atlantic and hide it in his attic. I had to go to war to understand. Only then did I realize what I had unleashed when I found that Kraut uniform in the attic—and why I deserved to be beaten silly for my actions.

During one of her long bullshit dinner lectures—which my son has many times privately told me I'm forbidden to critique—Hank's wife once said that in dreams and literature, the attic is a metaphor for the mind and a house is a metaphor for a person. The basement is supposed to be your subconscious. I don't know about the basement part, but rooting around in my father's attic is where I first found the key to his darker thoughts.

I still have the weapons I took off dead gooks. Proudest of a Colt .45, which I used to fire into the engines of enemy vehicles. One shot would stop a truck full of yellow men dead in its tracks. The guns I disassembled and sent home one piece at a time. The geniuses scanning the mail were too stupid to realize you could send an entire gun home that way. Military intelligence. Oxymoron. The US government didn't care about knives.

My civilian son will never understand these things.

My old man died in a lounge chair a few years back. Ninety-two years old. He was wearing the kelly-green Eagles tracksuit I had bought him, along with his favorite throwback Philadelphia A's ball cap, which reminded him of his youth when he played semi-pro baseball and the A's were still in our city. I saw my father through to the other side.

My father had bought the bullet a few days earlier. Called me up and said he was ready to die.

I said, "Okay."

He said he didn't want to go to the hospital. He didn't want any doctors involved, because he knew what liars and thieves they all are.

"Understood," I said.

Then I sat next to him as he died in his favorite chair—a

La-Z-Boy recliner. I paid a young, good-looking nurse to drip morphine under the old man's tongue so he wouldn't feel too bad as he went.

When he was still lucid, Father said, "Your son needs you. Your granddaughter needs you. Remember that mission."

They weren't there because they were in Hawaii on vacation and didn't want to spend the extra cash to fly home early, which tells you a little something about my son, but I understood what my father was saying, so I nodded.

Then I added the old man's World War II dog tags to my lucky Vietnam dog tags, rubber-banding the four of them together and then threading my silver chain through all four holes. I showed the old man.

He nodded.

I tucked them into my shirt.

He closed his eyes.

When the good-looking nurse began posing the million-dollar question with *her* eyes, I nodded again, which meant more morphine. Legal murder. Only no one will say it. It's supposed to be for the pain, but really you just help the dying overdose out of mercy. We made the decision without words. The little blonde was smart. Had murdered her share of old people already, and I admired her professionalism. If she had said the words, asked if we should kill my father, I'm not sure I would have been able to go through with what we both knew was the right thing to do. But she only asked with her eyes, which was classy and made the nodding easier. Helped me do my duty.

The old man whispered "Eve, Eve, Eve" for a while when he was morphine high. Barely audible. Eve was my mother's name. She died of a stroke several years before.

When the deed was done, I transferred my father's gold watch from his wrist to mine as the little blonde called the boys from the crematorium.

Two big guys finally showed up. One black. One white. The black guy had a panther tattooed on his neck. The white dude was pierced just about everywhere. His face looked like a fucking pincushion. Once they had my father on the stretcher and under the white sheet, I said, "Are you two Philadelphia sports fans?"

"Hell yeah!" the white one said.

The black guy just nodded enthusiastically.

"You like the Eagles, then?"

"Bleed green," the black guy said.

"Let me tell you something," I said, putting a finger in each of their faces. "The old man goes into the fire wearing the tracksuit and the hat. I catch either of you wearing my father's clothes, and I'll put a fucking blade through your esophagus and watch you choke on your own blood. Understood?"

I pulled out my military-issue switchblade I got off this Iraq and Afghanistan war vet I met at the VA. He was a true American hero, by the way. Three tours. Gave his legs for his country. He's got prosthetics now. Completes goddamn marathons on those things, and could still kick your two-legged ass in five seconds flat.

But the knife he gave me, you stick the handle between the

target's ribs and hit the button. A spring-loaded blade pops out and shoots into the heart, killing instantly. Imagine what it could do to a throat.

I hit the button.

The blade shot up into the air between us.

The white one said, "Yo, man," and then started talking about how people shit themselves when they die, which was supposed to prove he wouldn't steal my father's kelly-green Eagles tracksuit. As if this kid didn't have access to a washing machine.

I told him I didn't give a fuck about all that. "My father goes into the fire, *as is*."

"Got it," the spade said, and when I looked into his eyes, I knew he did. You can tell a lot by looking into a man's eyes. I liked this black dude. He was honest. He understood the importance of my father being cremated in his favorite outfit. He was gonna do the job right, I could tell, so I let him and the other clown take away my old man's corpse.

The next day I called my father at 6:30 a.m., like I had done for the past four decades, to discuss the day's newspaper headlines and the sorry state of the world over coffee.

I had momentarily forgotten my father was dead.

I remembered just as soon as his answering machine picked up. His voice was the same as always. He sounded welcoming and at ease and a little excited that someone had called.

"Leave a message at the beep!" my dead father said.

I didn't say anything on the tape, but I called back several times, just to hear the old man's voice. It was a strange thing to do, and it was hard to reconcile the fact that we had killed him with morphine the day before with the fact that his voice was so alive on the machine. I kept calling back just to hear it, over and over again. I couldn't stop.

Around ten, I went to his place and disconnected the machine. I threw it away just so I wouldn't be tempted to play the message again. I had his dog tags. I had his watch. There wasn't anything else I wanted, so I started stuffing trash bags, most of which were snatched up by the black ladies who worked at his retirement home. I have no idea what they did with all of my father's junk. I didn't care.

In my father's wallet I found three pictures.

A tight-lipped black-and-white head shot of his best friend from high school, George Esher, who parachuted out of a plane back in World War II and was never seen again.

A grainy picture of me on my wedding day. I'm in a dark-green tuxedo, wearing a huge velvet bow tie. Jessica's standing next to me, wearing a white dress and holding a bouquet of light-blue flowers. Hank was in her belly. But I don't want to talk about Jessica right now. I'll talk about Jessica later.

The third picture is my son, Hank, when he was playing Little League. Maybe ten years old. He's holding a wooden bat and wearing a navy cap and uniform. It's supposed to look like an official baseball card. The bat is resting on Hank's shoulder because he wasn't even strong enough to hold it up in the air for the time it took to snap a photo.

Your son and granddaughter need you, I heard my father echo once again from beyond the grave, and I knew it was true.

4.

June 6 was my father's favorite, favorite day of the year. After I got back from Vietnam, the old man opened up a little more about his wartime experience. Soldiers can talk to soldiers. D-day was his big day. The only thing he felt he did right in World War II. He lost a lot of time over there, and he got very emotional about it. But my father liked to recite General Eisenhower's D-day message:

> *Soldiers, Sailors, and Airmen of the Allied Expeditionary Force! You are about to embark upon the Great Crusade, toward which we have striven these many months. The eyes of the world are upon you. The hopes and prayers of liberty-loving people everywhere march with you.*

My old man knew the whole speech by heart. I think he had a drinking problem in World War II. I know he felt he had gotten men killed in an effort to secure booze. He never told me the whole story, but that's why he never drank once he came home. Not even a drop of alcohol. He was sober on D-day.

Your task will not be an easy one. Your enemy is well trained, well equipped and battle-hardened. He will fight savagely.

In the early eighties, I took my father back to the beach he stormed. The people of Normandy treated him like a hero. That's the only time I ever saw my father cry, in a little restaurant over there. The owner and head chef came out and thanked my father for his service. Everyone there stood up and applauded. It was a good moment. Maybe the best thing I ever did, taking him back to see the land he helped liberate from the fucking Nazis.

I have full confidence in your courage, devotion to duty and skill in battle. We will accept nothing less than full victory!

My father lost his watch storming Normandy. That was a little safe detail he'd tell civilians. Slid off somehow as he was making his landing. His father had given him the watch before he left for war as a sort of good-luck piece. The last time my old man saw his father's watch was on the boat that took him across the English Channel.

And so on the beach in Normandy, when his back was turned, I laid down a gold Rolex in the sand and said, "I think I found your watch!"

Father turned around fast, and the expression on his face was beautiful. He looked like a little kid who's heard the crack of his bat hitting the baseball, and somehow he knows he's just smacked his first home run.

"Eve, look!" he said to my mother. "I found my watch!"

The watch I bought him was the most expensive gift he had ever received from anyone, but he didn't even care about the monetary value. He wanted to stage photos of himself pretending to be shocked and then celebrating finding his watch, almost forty years after he miraculously survived a thick swarm of Nazi bullets. It was a good piece of theater. The happiest I ever saw my father. Best thing I ever did, taking him on that trip.

That night in the hotel, I heard a knock on my door around midnight.

I had been reading books about World War II so my father and I could have educated conversations. I envied my old man: he fought in a war that made sense afterward. I remember I was reading about Patton. That man was quotable. I was thinking about this fact when I heard the knock: "You're never beaten until you admit it."

I put on a robe and answered the door. My father was standing there, wearing pajamas and the gold Rolex. There were tears in his eyes. He didn't have to say anything—if you're battle-tested and you're with other battle-tested men, you never do. He reached out and put his rough, weathered hand on my shoulder. He nodded, and I nodded back. Mission accomplished.

My father loved seeing the people he liberated. Me, personally, I don't like the people my war tried to liberate.

My good buddy, who was over there in Vietnam when I was over there—who's now a multimillionaire many times over—

decided to go back, planned the whole trip, had the visas, hotel rooms, flights, everything else. He was just pushing me to go with him, go with him, go with him.

I was like, I can't, Frank; I can't. You don't understand. It's too emotional. Can't do it.

I never did go back, but Frank did. He loved it. He went all over on his return—Hanoi, Saigon, even into Cambodia to see the temples. But he was in a different situation than I was. He was company commander and had a construction crew over there, so he spent pretty much the whole tour building hospitals and schools and roads and stuff like that. What he did was positive. And he stayed in Nha Trang, a very nice French resort on the coast.

"Frank, you don't understand," I said. "When I was in Vietnam, I didn't stay in a hotel. I stayed in a jungle. I slept in trees. Ate canned food and snakes. Spent all my days killing people. What I wanna go back for? I got no good memories. You have a lot of good memories. I got *no* good memories. I want nothing to do with those people, or that place."

Plus, there was the memory of the bad shit I was ordered to do to that big Indian motherfucker, Clayton Fire Bear, but I'll explain all that later.

Regardless, I don't have a D-day.

Nowhere to visit.

5.

The second time my son, Hank, visited me in the hospital, he was a little more hospitable, so I asked him if he might bring my granddaughter for a visit. Like I said before, Ella and I have an understanding. But Hank said she was in Amsterdam with her bitch mother.

"When are they coming back?" I asked, which is when my son began crying again. I've never met a man who cries more than my son, and it never fails to alarm me. He wouldn't have lasted five minutes in the jungle. I saw a lot of men like Hank get killed quickly. They'd buy the bullet before they even began their tours, and that would make them a huge fucking liability.

I remember this one time we were assigned an FNG—Fucking New Guy. He looked like he was twelve and could hardly stand up with all his gear on. I don't even think his balls had dropped yet.

"You guys are going to make sure I don't die, right?" he said.

And he wasn't joking. There were tears in his eyes. He had bought the bullet on day fucking one. We all knew he'd be dead within hours, maybe minutes. Once you thought you were going to die, you did, and usually in a hurry. There was no reason to speak with him—he was already gone, and we didn't want Death to think we had anything to do with this bullet-buying FNG.

I glanced down at his brand-new boots, and they looked about my size. Mine were waterlogged and had a few holes. Fucking rice paddies. Jungle rot. The meat of my feet was literally falling off the bone.

"His boots are mine," I said to the rest of the men.

"Why are you claiming my boots?" the FNG asked in the voice of a little girl whose beloved cat is about to be put in a sack and drowned in a river.

No one answered him.

Everyone claimed different pieces of his gear as he spun around, looking for eye contact and begging any of us to speak with him. We knew acknowledging him in any way whatsoever was suicide, so we pretended he wasn't even there.

An hour later, a sniper shot him through his left eye. We returned fire, and no one else was wounded.

Now, why did the gook sniper pick the FNG?

Answer: he didn't. Death picked. The FNG had bought the bullet with his whimpering and fear. It was obvious. We were protected because we didn't engage with that sort of behavior.

I put on my new socks and boots and was grateful to be alive, glad that Death and I still had an understanding.

But my crying son, Hank, and I weren't in the Vietnam jungle; we were in a Jefferson Hospital room in Philadelphia. So I asked what happened with Femke.

That no-good foreign devil had tired of America and was

yearning for her motherland. Turns out Femke was also fucking another European on the side, a visiting professor from Amsterdam who specializes in bullshit global warming theories and breaking up marriages.

"You let her take your daughter out of the country?" I asked my son, because that was not good. Things got complicated once you were out of the United States, and I imagined fighting an international custody battle would be much easier if you actually had possession of the child here in the USA.

"She just took Ella," my son said, his eyes welling up. "I woke up last week, and they were both gone. Just like that."

Kidnapping.

Hank went on to say that he had never done anything wrong; he had never been mean to his wife, had done everything she had asked, had bought the house she wanted in her preferred neighborhood, the car she wanted, a wardrobe they couldn't afford—gave her everything she asked for, allowed her to send Ella to the private Friends school Femke had picked out, which was when I interrupted.

I told him his defense, outlined his entire problem. Women tire of men who give them anything and everything they want. They may think they like their men castrated, but every woman has needs, and it takes a wild stallion to satisfy. A tamed, broken, ball-less stud is no stud at all.

This man-to-man got Hank to cease crying for a second, long enough to call me crude and sexist. He couldn't resist bringing up his mother too.

I pitied my son, and I blamed myself for his troubles. Maybe I should have been harder on him. Maybe I should have made him play football when he was in high school instead of allowing him to spend so much time painting, like his mother used to do.

Jessica taught Hank how to sketch and paint just as soon as he could walk. They spent years together at the easel she set up in his bedroom. Hand over hand, Jessica tried to pass on her gifts to our son. And he was a good pupil. You have to give him that. He would do anything and everything my wife told him to do. And they painted brilliant pictures together, hand over hand—but the genius vanished from the canvas and paper whenever Jessica took her hand off Hank's. He knew he was talentless even when he was in elementary school, but he faked it for fifteen more years, even after his mother was gone. You have to admire his determination, if nothing else. Finally he admitted he didn't have his mother's gift, became an art dealer, and married a foreigner.

"It's funny," he said, as we sat in my hospital room. "I tried to do the opposite of everything you did, Dad, and yet here we are, both alone."

So I said, "We need to go to Amsterdam and get Ella back. I have some contacts who can get us guns once we're in country, and—"

"What the hell is wrong with you?"

"Don't you want Ella back?"

"Of course I do," he said, "but this isn't the sixties, and we're not in the Vietnam jungle. I don't solve my problems with violence! Most people don't."

My son makes asinine statements like this every single day, while men all over the globe kill and kill without mercy. Does

Hank not even watch the fucking news? Does he not realize he's free to spout all of the stupid, misinformed, unchallenged civilian rhetoric he constantly promotes *because* we have the biggest and best military in the world, and we have always killed our enemies? Every day. Funded by our tax dollars, by the way, which my son pays just like everyone else. Could he really be so fucking naive? Without the military we'd be speaking German or Russian or maybe even Japanese right now. Does my son have any idea what a Nazi or Communist regime would have done to Flower Power hand-holders like him?

Hank went over to the window and continued his sniffling. It was strange how much I pitied him. If he weren't mine, I probably would have despised Hank Granger, but he was the closest I'd ever get to producing an heir, and so my emotions continued to betray me.

"She's gone on hunger strike," he said, and I could tell he was happy about this fact by the way his voice lifted.

"Ella?" I asked.

"Yeah," he said.

Ella was seven years old at the time. The body needs vitamins and fuel at that age so it can grow properly, and so I expressed concern, which prompted my son to raise his voice again, saying he knew that and so did Femke, and that's why she was putting Ella on a plane back to Philadelphia immediately. So all of the boohooing was for nothing.

And that's just the sort of mother my daughter-in-law is. Her global-warming-professor sex romp through Europe trumped her maternal duties. Her husband's father was fighting for his life after brain surgery, and she's off fucking some overeducated Dutch weatherman. Part of me was happy, I admit, just to be rid of her, because there was no way she'd be coming back. Even Hank knew it. Or so we thought.

"I'd ask where I went wrong if I didn't already know your answer would be horribly offensive," Hank said.

I just nodded. There was nothing that needed saying anyway at that point. The facts spoke loudly enough. I was sorry for my son's pain, but I couldn't help thinking he had brought it on himself by picking a woman who was bound to betray him at the first sign of trouble or even boredom. I sniffed her out more than a decade ago. I didn't need to tell Hank I was right—he now knew. The kicker was, he hated me for being right all along because it made him doubt himself, mistrust his instincts and his rosy dumb-civilian worldview.

The next time Hank visited my hospital room, Ella joined him. She gave me a big hug and a kiss right away, which was good medicine, let me tell you—it'd been so many months since I last saw her. I told her I missed her like crazy, and she said she missed me "crazier," which produced a big-time fucking smile on my face.

Ella had lost a little weight. Her arms were a tiny bit thinner and her cheekbones were a little more prominent, and that made me want to put a bullet between her selfish mother's eyes, but I managed to keep those feelings to myself as Ella told me all about her solo trip across the Atlantic Ocean. She had sat next to a nice older lady—no doubt American—who shared her mints and even let Ella have the window when she had been assigned the aisle.

What type of mother puts her seven-year-old daughter on an international flight without adult supervision?

Ella was sitting on the edge of my hospital bed, holding my hand, telling me about the canals in Amsterdam, when she reached out and touched the bandage on my head. I asked if she wanted to see my scar, telling her the doctors had stapled it shut and you could still see the staples.

My pussy son protested, but I peeled the bandage off anyway.

"Whoa," she said, lifting her little eyebrows. And then she asked if I knew about her mother's new boyfriend.

"Your mother is a traitorous bitch, Ella. A real Jane Fonda," I said, which pissed off Hank, even though he knew I had spoken the truth. He kept blaming my cursing on the brain surgery, telling my granddaughter I couldn't help it, as if I never ever cursed before you people cracked open my skull and got me thinking so much about Clayton Fire Bear.

I don't think Ella understood what I had said anyway, because she started talking about Gandhi and nonviolence and not eating to get what she wanted from her mother, which, in this case, was to come home to the land of the free.

I once read that Gandhi used to sleep naked with his own teenage niece and force her to take baths with him. Apparently he beat his wife too. But I didn't want to talk with Ella about a wife-beating sexual deviant and how schoolteachers lie, so instead of setting the record straight on India's most famous pervert, I told her that I was just glad she was back in the best country in the entire world, the United States of America, and my little granddaughter nodded proudly, because she is a true patriot.

Then she said she was glad I was going to be living with them, which made me look over at my son, who explained I needed to be supervised for a time.

Ordinarily, I'd have told him to go fuck himself, but it was obvious that he needed me to help him put his life together after his wife had run out on him. Hank was going to need a hand with Ella and was just too shy and weak to ask directly for assistance. So I let that slide too, and told Ella I was very excited to be moving in with her.

"Do you want to stay in my room?" she said.

I told her I needed my own room because of the nightmares. I still sometimes wake up screaming, soaked in sweat. Ella said she had bad dreams too, so it was okay. I appreciated her trying to bond with me, but my granddaughter didn't understand a few things. Primarily that it's really fucking dangerous to interrupt my sleep, because I used to reflexively kill anything that woke me up in the jungle—rats, snakes, gooks, insane perverts (which I'll tell you about later), whatever the fuck. And that killer instinct remains strong to this day. Instead, I just told my granddaughter that I preferred my own room with a lock on the door and left it at that.

Hank watched us talking with this distant look on his face. We used to call it the thousand-yard stare back in Vietnam. Men got that when they had seen too much horrific shit or when they had simply given up, which was different than buying the bullet.

Regardless of all that, I knew my son's head was fucked, and here he was now, all alone with a seven-year-old daughter to take care of. My old man's dying words echoed in my head once more. It was clear that I had one last mission. And I always, always, *always* complete my mission.

6.

The first thing that happened when I moved into my son's house was this: Ella and I had a tea party. This was to welcome me, because my granddaughter is a hell of a lot more thoughtful than her foreigner mother. My son, Hank, did not attend.

Normally I don't have tea parties with little girls, but I made an exception because my granddaughter allowed me to have real coffee. So the tea party was just barely manly enough to be okay.

Ella drank pretend tea out of a pink plastic cup. Every time she took an imaginary sip, she stuck out her pinkie like she was the Queen of England. She was also wearing white gloves and a tiara made of rhinestones that sparkled like the thing was plugged in.

I was wearing my default safe outfit: camo pants, jacket, and bucket hat. We had stopped at my home on the way, so I was also packing heat again, which felt good, like coming up for air after diving deep down into the ocean, but my antigun son didn't know that I was carrying. Just a small Glock in an ankle holster. Nothing too serious. No AK-47 or anything like that. Left my bazooka at home. Didn't even bring my flamethrower.

"Why the hell are you in full camouflage?" Hank asked, because he didn't understand what it was like to be under attack and vulnerable. He didn't have a Clayton Fire Bear.

My nervous, untrusting son actually patted me down when we left my house, because he had banned me from carrying a firearm. "I'll allow you one knife only," Hank said, because I can't really sleep without a knife under my pillow. They had to knock me out with powerful drugs every night in the hospital, and my goddamn liver needed a break from all those extra chemicals. But Hank doesn't know about ankle holsters, because he's an ignorant gun-hating liberal.

To be fair, Hank lives in a safe neighborhood and has a state-of-the-art security system, which he said was the reason we wouldn't need to bring any guns, but if my year in the army taught me anything, it was this: you never fucking know.

"Do you have any imaginary friends, like Mr. Peanuts?" Ella said to me during our tea party, after she had introduced me to everyone.

Mr. Peanuts was an invisible elephant who liked his pretend tea strong and his pretend cookies peanut-flavored, hence the name Mr. Peanuts. He was allegedly seated to my right, but only Ella could see him. That was the deal with Mr. Peanuts. On my left was a real doll named Julietta who liked her tea "stronger than an elephant's" but was on a strict diet, so she ate no imaginary cookies and took no imaginary lumps of sugar, nor did she take imaginary milk. Julietta could not see Mr. Peanuts either, and therefore doubted his existence.

"I had a friend named Tao once," I said to Ella.

"Towel?" she said. "Like what you use to dry yourself after a bath? That was his name, *Towel*?"

"Close enough," I said. "He was Cambodian. They have moronic names over there. He couldn't read or write, so not even he knew how to spell it. I have no idea either. But I think it might have been T-A-O. That's my guess."

Then she asked why he couldn't read or write. Was he blind?

And I told her that Tao was poor. Too poor to go to school. His parents were farmers. But the Vietcong killed them.

She wanted to know why the Vietcong had killed Tao's parents, and so I told her the Vietcong were very bad people. Not nice. They killed by the thousands. She wanted to know who the Vietcong were, so I said, "Communists. Bad guys. Our enemy."

It was nice to see Ella so concerned for Tao. She was biting down on her lip and twirling her hair around her finger. My granddaughter is compassionate.

She wanted to know what Tao did after his parents were killed, so I told her he escaped. Lived in the jungle. Ate snakes to stay alive. He was amazingly resourceful. Would have been extremely successful had he been born in America. Maybe would have even made president. But he wasn't lucky as we are. He was born in a shithole country.

She said, "He *ate* snakes?"

So I said, "I did too. Tons of them."

That made her stick out her tongue and say, "Yuck!"

And she was right, because snake is one nasty fucking meal.

Then Ella said she didn't want to talk about eating snakes, and so I said I didn't either.

"So Towel was just imaginary?" Ella asked. "Like Mr. Peanuts?"

I didn't know how to answer that one. I met Tao when I was rogue in the jungle. I hadn't spoken to another American soldier for weeks. They say that after so many days in combat, every man is considered legally insane. That's when I met Tao. After so many days in combat. No breaks. Very little sleep. Constant danger. Ceaseless uncertainty for days and days.

I don't even really remember the first time Tao and I bumped into each other. I only remember spending a few weeks with him on the hunt. All he wanted to do was kill Vietnamese people to avenge the murder of his family and the destruction of his village. He killed Vietnamese by the dozens and with an unending supply of rage in his heart. Soldiers had raped his sisters and mother and made his father watch before they rounded everyone up and burned them all alive—everyone Tao had ever known went up in smoke. He saw the horror show from a tree he had climbed. The Vietcong never looked up, and that's why he was alive, or so the story went.

By the time we met, we were both all-stars when it came to killing Vietcong, so we were a fucking dream team. We killed dozens a day. And we collected gold for him, killing those who had it, because I knew Tao would sure as hell need it. I was leaving after my tour. Going back to the USA. He was stuck there in the shit and would have to bribe his way into a peaceful existence down the line, especially if the commies won.

The funny thing was that Tao only knew a limited amount of English, and I knew absolutely no Cambodian. Most of the time it was like we communicated telepathically, or maybe akin to a two-man pack of lions using pheromones. When a man is reduced to hunting and killing, words become useless—maybe even dangerous. Sometimes I felt as though we weren't even human anymore. Like we had evolved—or *devolved*, maybe.

Or maybe it was like when they bring in a Cuban or Dominican or a Jap or a Korean to play American baseball. The foreigner can't speak with his teammates so well, but they all know the rules of the game, so it doesn't matter once they're on the field.

When I really think about it, I remember Tao drawing pictures in the dirt with a stick to explain what happened to his village. It wasn't too hard for me to guess what the pictures meant. War is predictable in the absolute worst possible ways.

Our killing spree lasted maybe three or so weeks, and then one day I woke up in a tree and Tao was gone, along with the gold we had tied to high branches like goddamn monkey pirates.

A stateside military shrink who debriefed me confidentially —or so he said—back in Kansas in 1967 suggested that I made up Tao as a sort of alter ego, and while that sounded like a load of shit, I couldn't honestly argue that I was in my right mind during those three weeks. I can't even remember everything that happened. It was like a long, long, fucking long nightmare. When I try to conjure pictures and movies in my mind now, everything is blurry, like I'm trying to peer through a window that's been smeared with Vaseline.

"I had a dog in Vietnam for a time too. His name was Bullshit," I said to Ella, trying to change the subject, and that's when my son barged in and said the tea party was over.

"Why did you name your dog Bullshit?" Ella asked.

"Are you happy now?" Hank said to me. Nice little rich girls aren't supposed to say "bullshit," I guess. But I hadn't told Ella to say that word, I just told her the name of my dog in Vietnam. His name really was Bullshit. We even made him dog tags with BULLSHIT stamped into the metal.

"I'm tired," I said to Hank, and it was true. I was fucking exhausted after only a few hours walking around in civilization free again. "These meds have me feeling dizzy. I think I oughta lie down in my room."

"You do that," Hank said. As I made my way down the hall to the guest room, I overheard him telling Ella that I wasn't thinking straight and she couldn't believe everything I said. That they had to let my brain heal. And until that happened, she was supposed to think of my quote-unquote "stories" as "make-believe." My ignorant son actually said my Vietnam experience was like a fucking *fairy tale.*

I shook my head, because I began to realize that my brain surgery was going to be a convenient eraser for Hank. Anything cerebral I said from then on would be easily discredited because the government had cracked open my skull and taken a piece of my brain out. But what the fuck could I do about that? Nothing. So I laid myself down on the guest bed and thought about Bullshit.

I found Bullshit in the jungle. He was a high-spirited little mutt, and he ran right up to me, barking and jumping and wagging his tail. When I bent down, he licked my face all over, which is when I knew we were going to be buddies. I've always loved dogs. More than I like most *people*, even. And so I named the little guy Bullshit and took him back to the base with me.

Bullshit was a big hit. Everyone loved him. He got fat because so many of us were feeding him scraps. It was like the little guy died and went to USA heaven right there in Vietnam.

I had a lot of trouble sleeping in 'Nam, but when Bullshit was snuggled up with me I slept soundly through the night, maybe because he'd bark if anything came close, so I didn't have to keep one eye open all the fucking time. In the jungle you learn how to do that, by the way. You sleep, but you never *really* sleep. With Bullshit, I'd sleep on my side in the fetal position, and he'd curl up in the V between my shoulders and my knees. That was the best rest I ever got in Vietnam—maybe in my entire life.

I tried taking him on patrol with me in the jungle, but he barked too much and was always giving away our position, so that was no good. I had to leave him behind whenever I went out killing gooks. He didn't like that and would come looking for me, so I had to start locking him up or keeping him tied to a rope. I'd ask guys to feed him when I was gone, and that wasn't a problem at all, but it was hard to get anyone to keep him in a tent because he would eventually shit and piss in there, and no one wanted that. No one was about to walk a dog on a leash in the middle of a fucking war, and so eventually someone would untie Bullshit and let him out to do his business. A few times he'd dart off and find me in the jungle, which was never good.

The last time I left Bullshit alone, someone finally let him out to take a dump and he took off looking for me, but I never did see him alive again.

When I returned to the base, I called for him and he didn't come. I asked around, and the guys said they hadn't seen him for half a day or so.

I got a bad feeling. A lot of bad shit could happen to a little dog in the fucking jungle. There were giant snakes. King cobra. Pythons. Vipers. Nasty shit. Tigers. Land mines. Agent Orange. A million things that can kill your dog. Fucking punji-stick traps.

But my worst fear of all was that he had been eaten by gooks, because they love to eat dogs and were unmerciful killers. They'd soften the meat by beating the dog. Just tie it up and start whaling on it, breaking bones as the helpless little pup shrieked out in pain. They'd boil it alive after that. Those fucking people were supreme savages.

So I headed out into the jungle with a heavy heart, looking for Bullshit.

Soon I came across Ding-Dong, who, like I said before, owed me a favor. And so I told him that my dog was missing, and I wanted it back.

He looked at me like I was crazy, because in his mind being upset about a dog was like worrying about the well-being of a giant centipede or a mosquito. Gooks didn't give a shit about dogs, didn't understand the bond that happens between humans and canines. I've often wondered if that means they weren't really human themselves, but I know that's probably not a very politically correct thing to say these days. It was okay for our government to drop napalm on those fuckers for years and years, but God forbid I suggest that they ate dogs, which they absolutely did.

Ding-Dong loved being alive and he loved money even more, so I told him that I'd forget about the chicken blood on the VC uniforms he sold and give him a hundred US dollars if he found Bullshit. I gave a description—Bullshit was about twenty-five pounds and brown, hence the name—and let him know about the dog tags we put around his neck.

"Bullshit. Dog tags," Ding-Dong repeated, and then he was gone.

It only took him a few hours to find Bullshit.

Ding-Dong led me to a nearby village. A small gook child was wearing Bullshit's tags around his neck. His mother was in her hut, boiling my dog like he was a common chicken. When I approached her, she smiled and offered to feed me my dog. I handed Ding-Dong his money and told him to leave, which he did quickly. Once the gook woman understood what was about to happen, she began offering me her body, but I wasn't interested in sex that day.

What would you do if you knew gooks had beaten your dog and then tried to eat him?

Bullshit was my one comfort in a fucking nightmare, the only good thing that happened to me in Vietnam.

He might have been the best friend I have ever had in my entire life.

If you have a dog, I want you to think about him or her. Think about strangers tying your best friend up. Intentionally breaking his bones. Wearing his or her tags like a trophy afterward. Boiling alive and then eating your dog. It's un-American and goddamn inhumane.

How would you have righted that wrong?

I did what you would have done—what any rational dog-loving American would have done.

I made damn fucking sure that not a single one of those villagers ever ate another dog again.

Period.

I left devoid of ammunition and with flames licking the sky behind me. Then I wept alone in the jungle for Bullshit, too afraid to return to base because I didn't want my army brothers to see me crying like a fucking girly-man.

I don't remember much of what happened between that experience and my going AWOL, which followed quickly. I remember killing gooks with Tao. Stockpiling gold. Eating snakes. Shooting every face I saw, including monkey faces that popped out of the jungle. Anything with eyes, we killed.

But I don't remember specific details.

Maybe it's like the way you might remember going to a certain grocery store many times when you used to live in a certain town decades ago, but you don't remember the specific trips you took, or what exactly you purchased, or who you might have seen, or what was on sale. You just remember shopping at that store, but nothing else. You probably spent hundreds of dollars, purchased thousands of products even, but how specific can you be about any of it, really?

If something out of the ordinary happened—like maybe you dropped an egg on the floor, or you walked out without paying by mistake but were too embarrassed to go back in and so you just drove away, or maybe somebody armed and dangerous robbed the store while you were there, or a local celebrity happened to bump his shopping cart into yours—you might be able to recall a detail about one of those things because the experience would have been out of the ordinary. But what happens repetitively usually gets lost in the fog of our memories and is easily forgotten.

Killing people with Tao became my equivalent of going to the grocery store. To be honest, I remember the individual monkeys I wasted better than the gooks. I was always sorry when an animal caught a bullet. Animals don't understand war. They never killed my friends.

And I don't know why I'm remembering *this* all of a sudden, but it seems significant, so I'm just going to include it here and now. The last fight I got into with my wife happened just before she died, and it was about groceries. *Groceries.* Toward the end she was so mentally fucked up she couldn't even manage to keep food in our refrigerator, and she wasn't feeding our son when I wasn't home, although Hank would try to cover for her.

Anyway, on this particular night, I came home a little late from work. Young Hank was curled up on the sofa, hugging his knees. When I asked what he had eaten for after-school snack and dinner, he looked away. Then I heard his stomach growl, and I knew he hadn't eaten anything.

I looked in the fridge, and we didn't even have milk and bread; the cupboards were empty too, so I went out back and banged on Jessica's art studio door until she answered a few minutes later. Then I screamed at her until she cried. I told her she only had to feed the boy twice a day—because he bought school lunch—and make sure there was something in the cabinets for an after-school snack. That was her only responsibility in the world. I made all the money, paid all the bills, made sure she had art supplies so she could spend all her time painting. Jessica kept saying the fluorescent lights in the grocery store ceiling made her feel insane and that there were bad people there who were spying on her. Her mind had finally snapped, but I didn't want to believe it. I used my army training and tried to put the confidence in her by yelling. But of course that didn't work.

She fell to her knees and begged me not to make her go to the grocery store ever again.

"You have to contribute SOMETHING!" I yelled down at her in my frustration, and I think those words are what killed her, which makes me a murderer once again.

The funny thing is this: I took Hank to the grocery store that night, just before it closed, and I let him eat chips out of the bag before we paid for them, and zoom through the aisles using the cart as a race car. And I also let him buy whatever the fuck he wanted. We filled the entire cart and then we dined at home on sugar cereal after his bedtime on a school night while Jessica sobbed in her studio. It might have been the best night I ever had with Hank—the closest I ever felt to my son.

We didn't know what horrors were just around the corner. All the signs were there, but we chose to ignore the obvious.

I'd give my life in a heartbeat to go back in time and tell my wife she never had to go to the fucking grocery store again, and that her art was the best contribution to the family that she could ever make.

But I can't do that.

So I have to live with my civilian guilt too.

7.

I may deploy colorful language from time to time, but *I am not* a racist, *nor* am I a bigot, despite what my son says about me.

Because he doesn't know shit about my life, Hank's eyes fell out of his dumb liberal head when my good friend Sue Wilkerson came over to his house one night for dinner.

Sue is genetically Vietnamese, although she is mentally American with a real red, white, and blue heart, on account of her being raised here in the United States by a Vietnam veteran named Alan Wilkerson, whom I respect unequivocally.

Ten or so years into postwar civilian life, Alan decided to rescue an orphan from Vietnam. Maybe he got to feeling sorry about whatever the fuck he had done in the war. That was none of my business, so I didn't ask him. Just an educated guess on my part. No one went into the jungle and came out clean. That's a given. If you were there, you did exactly what all of the rest of us did to survive, which wasn't pretty.

What Alan told me was this: he didn't want to procreate himself, because he'd been exposed to too much Agent Orange and therefore was afraid of impregnating his wife with a genetically altered baby. If a man's sperm supply is supposed to look like sunny-side-up eggs, Agent Orange sticks a fork into the scrotum and makes scrambled. Basically, that nasty batch of chemicals is a wild card. We still don't know exactly what the fuck Agent Orange does to human beings, because our government is run by cowards. But we do know that Alan's fear is one hundred percent warranted.

There are a lot of people here in the States, and even more in Vietnam, who are grotesquely deformed because of that shit the US government and motherfucking moron politicians made us spray everywhere. Kids born with four arms and no legs. Two torsos attached together at the belly button. Elongated alien heads. Bulging eyes. Nightmare shit. Just type "Agent Orange Babies" into the Internet. You'll see the horrors that men in three-piece suits with no fucking understanding of war can unleash from a stateside desk.

They told us it was perfectly safe. Wouldn't hurt humans. Our sperm would not mutate. Fuck them. Every American politician during the Vietnam War who said Agent Orange was harmless should be forced to gargle with it until their tonsils glow.

I truly feel bad for the fucked-up kids in Vietnam, but those people were mostly the enemy. The American Vietnam vets whose kids have inherited problems related to Agent Orange—those heroes should be given millions by the US government. But Uncle Sam is exceptional when it comes to fucking over vets. His screwing-veterans record is impeccable, and yet he never seems to have any trouble getting new recruits.

BE ALL YOU CAN BE.
ARMY OF ONE.
ARMY STRONG.

Can anyone tell you what those slogans actually mean?

Doesn't matter.

No one really gives a single shit about these things, I'm aware, but I have to keep saying all this anyway until the day I die. Too many American patriots and heroes have gotten fucked in the ass by Uncle Sam, who to this day is still doing a lot of ass-fucking when it comes to our psychologically and/or physically wounded veterans. If you don't believe me or think I am exaggerating, visit your local VA. The horror show is on display daily. But you won't go. No one goes. No one cares.

I met Sue in spin class over in the city. I like spin class. Lots of hot, tight young female bodies in spandex. Great workout too. None better.

My spin class instructor is named Timmy. He's off-the-charts gay, definitely the woman in his gay homo relationship, and so I call him Gay Timmy. But before you go stereotyping against him, believe me when I say he has the body of a Navy SEAL. You would not want to fight this gay motherfucker, trust me. You might think I hate the gays because I was in the army and am a registered Republican, but you'd be dead fucking wrong. I respect those people.

Gays always contribute something positive to the community. You never see gays move into a neighborhood and make it worse. No, you always see them renovating old fucked-up houses, adding value, making things look better, starting businesses.

Don't get me wrong. I could never willingly hold hands with another dude, let alone put another man's dick inside of me. No homo here. Heterosexual and proud of it. I'd march if we straights had a parade.

But consenting adults can do whatever the fuck they want to each other as far as I'm concerned. That's what freedom means. And Timmy is the best spin class instructor in the city. You have to sign up for his class years in advance or know someone who can get you in if you want the privilege, and believe me when I say it absolutely *is* a privilege.

I have driven BMW for decades and own—outright, no mortgage—a South Jersey suburban house valued well over eight hundred thousand. I've made many millions in my lifetime—but the truth is that most people are more impressed with my spot in Gay Timmy's spin class. That's how much respect this exceptionally fit homo commands.

I did some noteworthy real estate transactions with Timmy's homo lover, who is a big-time player in the Philly real estate game and the man in their gay relationship. The gays only say "life partner" instead of "homo lover" to people they think are uncomfortable with their gay lifestyles, by the way, and I'm comfortable, so I can say "homo lover." I've been given clearance, if you're one of those uptight liberals who keeps track of these things.

Anyway, Gay Johnny and I each made seven figures on this old building I purchased back in the eighties. Johnny turned my shithole property into a hot popular brewpub down in Old

City maybe eight years ago. Big, big, *big* fucking coin was made by all parties involved. Win, win, win. So we're tight, Johnny and yours truly. Anyone who helps me make serious money is okay in my book, no matter where he may or may not insert his dick.

Here's another good thing about homos. They are extremely thoughtful and surprisingly patriotic. Since I've known them, Johnny and Timmy have sent me a card every year on Veterans Day, thanking me for my service. And there is always a little notice stating that they donated money to a charity that supports US veterans. They donate in my name too, which is a nice touch, even though they get to keep the tax write-off for themselves. My favorite gay couple hasn't missed a single year yet. They have no idea what the fuck thanking me for my service means, because they have never been to war, but I appreciate the sentiment. Actually goes a long way with me, especially when I consider how many heterosexuals say fucking zilch to me on Veterans Day, let alone make a donation to help my brothers-in-arms.

So these two are okay in my book. Any day of the week, I'll take a classy pair of gays who say "Thank you for your service" over a million straight ignorant assholes who say nothing at all to combat veterans. The gays can hump each other all they want as long as they are patriotic, because that's true American freedom. Love your country. Period. And Timmy and Johnny proudly fly the stars and stripes from their home on historic Elfreth's Alley, which is a detail not lost on me.

Any fucking way, I'm in Gay Timmy's spin class, riding the bike, sweating my motherfucking nuts off, when I smell nuoc mam, which is a Vietnamese fish sauce.

Fucking nasty awful stuff. Make you wanna puke, just smelling it.

I scanned the room using the mirrors on the walls and found the culprit pretty easily. There was this little Vietnamese broad toward the front pedaling fiercely, sweating up a goddamn rice-paddy monsoon. The fish sauce smell had to be coming through her pores, no doubt, I initially thought.

This fucked up my spin class experience, to say the least. Timmy kept saying, "Keep pedaling, David! You can do it! Beauty is paid for in sweat!" because my ass was dragging. He usually doesn't have to single me out like that. I generally can keep up, because I am a tough motherfucker and don't you forget it. So he knew there was something wrong right away when he saw me putting in a subpar spin.

What Timmy didn't understand was this: Back in Vietnam, I used to set up with a sniper rifle downwind of a trail. I'd smell the gooks before I ever saw them. I don't have miraculous powers when it comes to my nose. But nuoc mam stinks. Fucking hell, it's a truly terrible potion. You can smell it from *miles* away. Eat that stuff, and it's like you sweat rancid putrid liquefied fish guts for days. The little bastards in Vietnam love that shit too. Drink it down by the bottle. And whenever I got a whiff of it during my tour, that meant I was going to do some killing. So you can imagine what the scent of nuoc mam does to my brain when it comes to triggers and flashbacks here in the USA. Takes me right back to the jungle.

"Get that ass up in the air, David!" Timmy yelled at me. "Pedal like your life depends on it!"

Timmy was pushing me like he was paid to do, because

he is an extraordinary motivator when it comes to fitness, but he didn't know that I was in kill mode at the time. Civilians don't understand kill mode because that switch in their brain has never been activated. So I didn't blame Timmy. He didn't know any better. Instead, I just got off my bike and hit the shower early. I gave Timmy a wave on the way out, letting him know I was okay, but he looked concerned nonetheless.

Gays are pretty perceptive when it comes to feelings, which is another thing I admire about them. If ever I'm sending flowers to someone, I always make sure I hire a gay florist. You'd have to be a fucking moron to hire a straight man to arrange flowers. Gays are *the best* when it comes to floral arrangements. I regularly send flowers to Geraldine, my old secretary from my banking days, because she's a classy lady and her husband, Carl, died a few years ago, so he obviously can't send her flowers anymore. Geraldine is black, by the way—if you couldn't tell by the name—and what racist sends a black lady flowers multiple times a year, let alone hires a black secretary in the eighties? I'd like to see my liberal son go back in time and hire a black before it became the trend. People praise you for hiring blacks today. You were punished, back in my day.

And if you're thinking, How the hell did the foulmouthed son of a bitch telling you this story ever make it in the banking world? you don't understand real estate investment. I wasn't a born-rich New York banker in a ten-thousand-dollar suit getting cute little manicures during Friday lunch breaks so I'd look refined in the Hamptons on the weekend. I was a Philly banker kicking ass on my city's streets. Hustling. Making prime-time players real money. And if you make money for the right sort of men, you can do and say pretty much whatever the fuck you want.

After I showered and dressed, I waited around for spin class to end because I didn't want to offend Timmy and get kicked out of the best class in the city, nor did I want to risk offending Johnny, with whom I hoped to make a lot more money in the future. It's been my experience that if you offend one gay, you offend them all. They stick together, so you have to be careful. I never want to be on the wrong side of a queer parade because there is no fucking end to a gay political movement once they get their minds made up, which is another thing I admire about them. They are a strong people with a rock-solid resolve. Don't fuck with the gays. Trust me.

So I'm standing there outside the class when it ends and everyone starts leaving the room, headed for the showers, except the little Vietnamese lady. She's talking to Timmy, and they keep touching each other's arms like gays and women do when they are close, which is when I realized that the gook must be friends with Timmy. I figured she was probably okay if she was Gay Timmy's personal acquaintance, but I wasn't sure I could control myself if I got another strong whiff of the mind-altering gook condiment known as nuoc mam.

Just as soon as I turned away, trying to avoid an awkward and potentially dangerous situation—trying to "de-escalate," as my VA shrink says—Timmy calls my name and says he wants to introduce me to his "good friend."

I was in a tough fucking situation there. The scent of nuoc mam in my nose is like pressing the button that launches a nuclear warhead, and I knew it. But I also really loved this spin class, and gays can be super touchy when it comes to social etiquette. If I walked away, I couldn't exactly call Timmy later and say "I was afraid I'd kill your gook friend who smelled like nuoc mam." No one is going to understand and condone that sentence unless they were in the Vietnam jungle back in the sixties. And certainly not Timmy, who has thrown people out of his class *permanently* for walking in thirty seconds late. You do not fuck with Timmy once you "make the commitment" to be in his "spinning family." That room full of spin bikes is *his* domain. Where *he* gets to be God, and I respect that. I had made the commitment.

The last time I stopped going to spin class, I gained twenty pounds and had a heart attack, which forced me to give the thieving doctors big-time money, so I couldn't afford to even accidentally insult Timmy, who was literally keeping me alive at that point in my life.

All of this led to me trying to hold my breath as I walked back into the spinning room, but of course, eventually I needed more air.

I could still smell traces of nuoc mam, but the scent was much fainter, which sort of disproved my theory about it being the gook whose pores were venting that vile fish sauce.

"David," Timmy said, "I'd like you to meet my good friend Sue Wilkerson. Sue, this is David Granger."

Sue stuck out her little yellow hand, and because of my respect for Gay Timmy I shook it. As our hands went up and down in between us, I got a whiff of her. I braced myself for a violent outburst, but there was no nuoc mam in the air. Instead, I got a nose full of vanilla with maybe a hint of lavender.

"You smell surprisingly nice," I said.

"*Surprisingly*?" Timmy said, in a way that let me know I had violated one of his many secret homo rules. An agitated gay is a lot like a king cobra rising up, flaring its hood, and hissing at you. Yes, the cobra can kill you. But the dramatic reaction is just a warning, and there is never a problem if you back down. Gays are peaceful by nature, and I had learned this long ago.

So I said to Timmy, "After an intense workout, I always stink like shit." And then to Sue I said, "I can see you're Vietnamese."

"I am," she said. "And I'm impressed. Most Americans think every Asian person is Chinese."

"Yeah, well, I'm not a fucking racist," I told her, "and I spent some time in Vietnam. A few decades back. Before you were born. And today's average American civilian is a moron anyway."

Sue laughed in this confident and easy way that I immediately liked, and then she told me that her father was a Vietnam vet.

So I said, "I hope he wasn't Vietcong."

But it turns out her father was US Army and white. She had been adopted. So I immediately told her to thank her father for his service, on my behalf.

"I'm sure he'll thank you for yours too," she said. Letting me know Timmy had already told her I was a veteran, just like her father.

Timmy chimed in here and said, "David, you should meet Sue's dad. We'll have you all over for dinner. How does that sound?"

I don't know if you have ever gone to a gay dinner party, but let me tell you something—they are intense and last for fucking ever. I always end up taking too many cigarette breaks outside alone, and I often have to leave early because trying to keep up with lively gay dinner-party conversation makes me so fucking tired. On the plus side, I always enjoy speaking with my fellow Vietnam veterans, and this Sue Wilkerson had me curious.

This next statement will piss off the liberals for sure, but there is a big difference between a gook and a genetically Vietnamese woman raised here in the United States of America by a US Army veteran. Sue is as American as can be. Just like I'm not Irish or German or English, even though my Irish, German, and English ancestors passed down their genes to me. When you are raised in the USA and act like it, you are American, which makes you the best type of person in the entire world.

I've often wondered exactly what spin class attendee had eaten nuoc mam on the day that I met Sue Wilkerson. The rest of the people in that class were white, which probably meant that the nuoc mam eater had dined at a trendy Vietnamese restaurant prior to entering Gay Timmy's domain.

I wondered if a Caucasian could actually enjoy nuoc mam. Was that even fucking possible? I was betting no, because of the genes gooks have, which make their tongues different than ours. But I never did find out the answer to that little mystery, because I wasn't about to conduct a fucking survey. There was no good way to explain to the entire spin class why I wanted to know who was eating nuoc mam without getting into everything I'm telling you here, which is not exactly for the ears of the general public, to say the fucking least.

Anyway, Timmy and Johnny had that dinner party. Alan and I hit it off big-time, as you might imagine we would. He was a smoker too. Had downgraded to Marlboro Lights, just like me, but unlike me, he still had his lucky Zippo from the war, which was inscribed with the same exact words that were on my lucky lighter, which I lost somehow when I went rogue with Tao. It was a pretty common saying back in Vietnam, so the odds of us having the same Zippo weren't that amazing, but even still, the match was good enough for me. Here's the little Zippo-size poem:

WE ARE THE
UNWILLING
LED BY THE
UNQUALIFIED
DOING THE
UNECESSARY
FOR THE
UNGRATEFUL

Once I saw that lighter, I knew Alan was a true brother. He understood. And he became one of my closest friends. All because two homos were thoughtful enough to throw a dinner party for veterans.

And the more I saw of Alan, the more I saw of Sue, because she and her father were close. She started arranging outings for their family and me—fishing trips, weekend getaways, target practice at the gun range, stuff like that—and it all seemed completely normal. We also started eating a lot of meals together—Sue, Alan, his wife, and me. I didn't think too much about any of this until one night when I was smoking my last cigarette of the day on an Ocean City front porch, under a green awning attached to the house we had rented a few blocks away from the beach. Sue came outside and just started talking about how I made her father feel comfortable, and how she had never seen him so at ease in her entire life.

I told her combat veterans can only ever really trust other combat veterans.

Then she said, "My dad's never really had a friend before. As long as I've known him. I'm glad he has a friend now." Sue kissed me on the cheek. "Thanks," she added, before she went to bed.

Besides the business contacts I had made millions for, not too many people have said thank you to me and meant it. I knew Sue was special right then and there. I was damn lucky to have her in my life. And as I puffed on my cigarette under that Ocean City awning, I thought that sometimes just showing up consistently is enough to get the job done.

Unfortunately, Alan's wife died not too long after that conversation. Was hit by a taxi when she was crossing Market Street in broad daylight at City Hall. Fucking tragedy. The taxi driver was a Muslim, by the way. But not an asshole jihadist, according to the papers, who painted him out to be a nice family man. The brakes had gone. Freak accident. Or maybe someone had tampered with them, I don't know. But the police said it wasn't the Muslim's fault. He and his family came to the funeral, and he sobbed the whole time, which made me feel something for him even though he was a Muslim. Maybe it was because he was wearing a suit, like a proper American, instead of a bin Laden desert bathrobe. His family actually seemed nice too. The women covered their heads with colorful scarves, but they didn't cover their faces with those black torture devices that only show the eyes, which was an improvement, at least.

None of that mattered much to Alan, of course.

Good or bad Muslim, accident or murder, his wife was dead.

Then my worst fear for Alan came true. He started spending entire days stumbling around his house half drunk, mumbling all sorts of depressing awful things about how he wanted to die. In spite of the fact that he had an amazing daughter to live for, Alan bought the bullet because his wife, Shelly, had been the great true love of his life. She was the one who had kept him level regarding all the Vietnam shit. Saved his life when he came back from the jungle and then gave him the civilian life he didn't think was possible. She did all the legwork when they adopted Sue. And adopting Sue was smart. Gave Alan closure in a weird way. Allowed him to turn something bad into something positive. Intelligent woman. Shelly was a goddamn saint, just like my dead wife, Jessica.

Less than a year after I met him—and only a few weeks after we buried his wife—my Vietnam War buddy was diagnosed with stage IV lung cancer, which did not surprise me at all, because like I said before, he had bought the bullet. He got his wish and died shortly after getting that death sentence. The Grim Reaper is an efficient motherfucker. Give him an inch to work with, and it's lights out.

When he was on his deathbed, Alan asked me to watch over his daughter, and I, of course, said it would be an honor. I'd do just about anything for a fellow Vietnam veteran. And I wasn't about to buy the bullet anytime soon.

Sue got real lonely and depressed after her parents were gone. Took it hard because she didn't have too much experience with death.

Alan died a few months before my son disowned me at the Phillies game. I'm still upset about wasting such good seats right behind home plate, not that my highbrow son would care about something as lowly and common as professional sports. The prime view would have been wasted on him even if we had actually stayed to watch the remaining innings. But anyway, after all that had happened, Sue and I were both in need of a family.

We started going to the Ritz Movie Theatres together a few times a week to watch cerebral art-house films, which we both enjoy. We'd always have dinner—never Vietnamese food, no fucking nasty nuoc mam—afterward and discuss the flick. Sue would say I reminded her of her father. Like how I was always accidentally falling asleep during the movie, and Sue would worry about whether she should wake me up or not. And how she sometimes had to remind me what certain dishes were, especially at Italian places, because of my fucked-up brain, only we didn't know I had the tumor back then. And how I was always getting food on my shirt when I ate. She would say she used to call her dad Menu Man, because you could tell what was on the menu by reading the stains on his breast pockets. When she started calling me Menu Man, the significance was not lost on yours truly. And I'd tell Sue she was the absolute best Vietnamese person I had ever met, hands down, which made her smile sadly, because her genes would always make her a little sympathetic toward the little bastards in Vietnam, no matter how American she was at heart. I understood and accepted that fact. Let it slide, because Sue was value added.

Despite the other fact that she was always up my ass about my smoking, trying to get me to quit—she didn't understand that the cigarettes hadn't killed her father, his buying the bullet is what killed him—we became sort of close, and I consider Sue to be family now. She was there for me when my son wasn't. She did a lot for me, like driving me to the hospital when I was too sick to get behind the wheel without killing anyone, back when my BMW was totaled anyway. Whenever I told her I felt bad wasting her time, she'd say she wished she could do all of this for her own parents, but she couldn't because they were dead. I was all she had left, and she was all I had. So she helped me get my medication at the store and sort it into that Sunday-through-Saturday pillbox for idiots like me. She made sure there was food to eat in my refrigerator. She kept me company. And she was also the one who made me call Hank after the operation. She would have tried to get me to call him before I went under the knife, but I tricked her into thinking he was in Europe and couldn't make it back in time, and that he knew already, which made Sue hate Hank until I told her the truth about my keeping the brain problems from my son because I was so fucking pissed at him.

The extra drugs they gave me at the hospital after they opened my skull made me softer than usual, and Sue used the sneaky part of her Asian heritage, took advantage of my incapacitated state, and cracked the case, which—I can see in retrospect—was what brought Hank and me back together in the end, so I guess I'm now grateful.

Hank doesn't know it, but I've even written Sue into my will. Behind Ella, Sue might be my favorite woman alive. Jessica remains my favorite woman, living or dead. I still love my dead wife even more than I love Ella, although Ella is a close second. Before I took out that telephone pole with my BMW and my head got all fucked up, I was starting to love Sue more than I loved Hank, who had abandoned me in favor of a Dutch cunt. It gives me no joy admitting that now, but it's true.

One of Sue's best attributes is that she is kind. Despite all I confided in her about my dumb liberal son, that little yellow woman was always thinking of Hank, trying to get me to look at things from his point of view, moronic as it was. Even Sue agreed my son could be one hell of a stubborn idiot. But Sue has a big heart, which reminds me a lot of my Jessica.

8.

So I was supposed to tell you about Hank meeting Sue for the first time, but I got sidetracked. These brain meds they have me on are brutal. It's hard to stick to just one train of thought, so I apologize for my past and future offenses.

I invited Sue over for one of Hank's "nutritional" and "fair trade" and "certified organic" dinners, which are often completely devoid of meat and bread and anything that tastes good at all. My son makes mashed potatoes with cauliflower, for Christ's sake. There are no potatoes in his mashed potatoes. No butter either. What the fuck? I asked him what could possibly be wrong with potatoes, which grow in the ground naturally—keeping the Irish alive for centuries—and he said they are high in carbs and then implied that I was fat, only he said it in a politically correct way. According to my son, I am "not heart-healthy." I prefer "fat" to "not heart-healthy." And I prefer potatoes to fucking cauliflower.

But dazzling Sue's taste buds wasn't even the secondary goal of the evening. If I wanted her to eat well, we would have gone out for a good steak at the Union League, where I've been a member for decades, because that patriotic society is pro-veteran and dedicated to the policies of Abraham Lincoln, who was a Republican, by the way. The current liberal party, who wants to enslave us all, did not emancipate the blacks. Republicans did that. They serve potatoes at the Union League too. I love potatoes with bacon and sour cream and chives and ketchup. That's *real* eating. But back to the goals of the evening. Like I was saying earlier.

First, I wanted to prove to my son once and for all that I was neither a misogynist nor a fucking racist. Having a woman who was also genetically Vietnamese for a best friend was my trump card. Two birds. One stone. I knew Hank couldn't say shit to me anymore about my colorful language once he'd met Sue, who fully accepts me for who I am, warts and all. And that's true equality, by the way, because Hank and Femke often acted like elitist snobs. Despite being so-called liberals, they looked down their noses at and hated more people than anyone I ever met.

The second part of my plan doubled down on the fact that I am no lousy fucking racist. Sue is a nice-looking and smart lady who is just about my son's age, give or take ten years. And she's a trillion times better than Femke. Femke was cold as ice on your balls, where Sue was like warm South China Sea sand between your toes. I wouldn't mind one bit having Sue for a daughter-in-law. I knew she'd be a big hit with Ella, and I was right about that too.

Sue came in with flowers for Hank and fun balloons for Ella, who hugged Sue right off the bat. The balloons had some cartoon princess on them that I couldn't identify, but apparently Ella could. I know because my granddaughter started jumping up and down like she had a firecracker up her ass just as soon as she recognized the princess. Already I could see that Sue would be a good mother for my granddaughter because she knew about the things Ella likes, and also Sue is thoughtful, having been raised by a fellow Vietnam veteran and his classy American wife. Most morons don't have enough class to bring anything to a dinner party. Pay attention, and you can spot a moron a mile away.

Like I said before, Hank's eyes popped out of his fucking skull when he saw Sue standing in his living room. It was a hilarious sight, because I knew he wanted to say *I never thought I'd see the day when my racist father would bring a Vietnamese woman to dinner*, but then he would have to admit that he was wrong about me all along and that would make *him* look like the bigot, which he wouldn't want to do, especially in front of a nonwhite.

"You must be Hank," Sue said once it was clear that my son was just going to stand there holding his dick.

"Actually, my name is Henri," he said, pronouncing it with a French accent, *Ahn-ree*. And then he added that his mother had named him after Henri Rousseau. He went on to say that only his father calls him Hank, because his father doesn't like the French.

Admittedly, the French are a hard race for this American patriot to like, because they let the Nazis take over their country and fucked up Vietnam before we got there too, but the point is this: My son never ever misses a chance to paint his father out to be a racist. He even tries to make me sound racist against other subsets of white people, like the French! I kept my mouth shut here and kept my mind on the greater good that I was trying to accomplish that evening.

"I'm not sure I know Henri Rousseau," Sue said, which did not impress Hank one bit, let me tell you, but he jumped at the chance to advertise his useless encyclopedic knowledge of dead non-American artists.

"He was a self-taught French painter," Hank said with unearned schoolboy pride, happy to supply all the art facts that our guest didn't already possess between her ears. It was like he was trying to win a prize. "Late nineteenth, early twentieth century. We have a really good Rousseau in the Philadelphia Museum of Art. *Carnival Evening*."

"Hank's mother was a painter. And a damn good one," I said, trying to knock my son off his professor podium before he launched into an art history lecture.

"Not that I'd know," Hank said, "because I never saw a single one of her paintings."

"Why's that?" Sue said.

Hank and I looked at our feet here, each of us daring the other to speak. It was just like Hank to bring up an uncomfortable topic when he should have been making our guest feel at home. Our answers to Sue's question would have been very different. Regarding Hank's mother, I'll tell you my version—aka the truth—before we finish here, but neither my son nor I wanted to talk about Jessica right then in front of Sue, and I don't feel like talking about my dead wife's notorious suicide just yet either.

Our guest broke the awkward silence. "Well, I'm Sue, and I've heard a lot about you, Henri."

"I'm sure you have," Hank said as he took the flowers, shook Sue's hand, and gave her body a quick once-over that neither Sue nor I missed.

Thanks to Gay Timmy, Sue had one of the top female bodies in all of Philadelphia. It helps that she was also Vietnamese, as those women are much less likely to become fat, even when they put down the fucking chopsticks and start eating real American food. Anyway, I could tell that my son had felt a little twinge in his pants, which meant the night had started out perfectly.

"Do you want to see my room?" Ella said and then dragged Sue up the stairs by the hand. Ella loves showing people her room. I have no idea why, as it looks like a regular pink-and-purple little-girl room, which is painfully uninteresting to anyone who is not a little girl. Sue was too polite to say as much, so up the stairs she went.

Once the women and children were out of earshot, Hank said to me, "You're full of surprises tonight, Dad."

So I told him that Sue had become my daughter. I pointed up to Sue on the second floor to support my case. Then I outlined all that she had been doing for me—a fucking long list—which was exactly what Hank was supposed to have done as my son. Any real American man would have felt immense shame, but not Hank. He probably thought he had done good stepping aside so that a minority *and* a woman could have his job as my child.

In response, Hank just added another place setting to the

table. Next he put some water into a fancy crystal vase and arranged the flowers Sue had given him. His arrangement looked like shit, because my son is a heterosexual.

I said, "I saw you give Sue the once-over."

"Please," Hank said.

"You telling me a liberal like yourself won't admit to being attracted to a woman of Vietnamese ancestry? I'm shocked. I thought you quote didn't see race unquote."

Then Hank said, "She's attractive, Dad. Anyone can see that. Racists and liberals alike."

My son was always dividing the world into two categories: liberals and everyone else, all of whom in his view were stupid and worthless and offensive.

"What?" I said. "You're too good to marry a Vietnamese woman?"

Hank shook his head here and laughed with college-scholarship-boy swagger. Then he said, "I'm already married, remember?"

It was hard to see the level of denial my son was exhibiting. I was embarrassed for him.

I was just about to ask Hank if he really thought Femke was ever coming back to America, but Ella descended the stairs still holding Sue's hand.

"I wanted to introduce Ms. Sue to Mr. Peanuts, but I couldn't find him!" Ella said. "He's vanished again!"

"You have a beautiful house," Sue said to Hank.

"Thank you," Hank said. "My wife did all the decorating."

"Ex-wife," I said. "She's long gone. Ancient history. Good riddance too."

Hank looked over at Ella without moving his head and then said, "Please, Dad."

"I know that Mommy has a boyfriend," Ella said to Hank. "Maybe you should have a girlfriend. That would only be fair."

"I agree," I said, backing up my granddaughter.

"Wine?" Hank said.

"Please," Sue answered.

"Can't drink," I said.

"We can have Perrier with lemon juice!" Ella said.

It was moments like this that I worried for Ella. What normal American seven-year-old drinks Perrier?

"Your xenophobic grandfather doesn't drink anything that doesn't have an American name, let alone a *French* soft drink," Hank said and then gave Sue a glance that made me realize he had mistaken my friend for a snooty elitist likely to laugh at his snide jokes. My stereotyping son always assumes that non-white people are Obama supporters, which is not the fucking case, and he'd know that if he ever bothered to go out into the world beyond his bubble of morons. Sue voted for McCain *and* Romney.

Sue smiled back at Hank because she is polite and my son has his mother's genes, which means he is attractive. I was counting on Hank's appearance to compensate for his misinformed worldview. Maybe that would be enough to woo Sue and get her interested in being Ella's new mother.

I don't approve of the way my son eats, but he is fit and looks like one of those model guys who fall out of the Sunday paper wearing nothing but tighty-whitey underwear and smug looks on their faces. The ones with their hands always behind their heads so you can see their shaved armpits. Those stupid advertising inserts no one wants. I think those underwear guys look like fucking assholes, but secretly I also want to look like them, which is why I spin with Gay Timmy, who has probably done some underwear modeling himself. But while I am an old man whose head-turning days are done, my son is still relatively young, in his mid-forties.

Soon we were all seated at the table, and Hank served something called Caprese Lasagna, which was basically tomatoes, fresh mozzarella, and basil wrapped in gluten-free noodles. I knew they were gluten-free because my son told us ten thousand times. I had eaten Italian food before with Sue, so I wasn't too worried about her enjoying the meal, especially since younger people generally seem to think my son can actually cook, despite the fact that he cooks pussy un-American dishes. But my hands were sweating the whole time we ate.

At some point Sue asked about the huge painting hanging in the dining room. A shit-eating grin bloomed on Hank's face, and then my son stepped up to his college-professor podium again.

Before I tell you about this painting, allow me to state that if I hung this one in my house tonight, Hank would disown me the second he saw it. You have to be a bleeding-heart liberal to get away with owning one of these.

It was painted by one of Hank's top moneymakers—an artist who goes by the name Eggplant X. That's this fucking clown's nom de guerre. *Eggplant X*. If I had come up with that shit, Hank would have snorted at me and called me a million insults.

The painting is a cartoon characterization of an old American stereotype. It's a little black boy eating a watermelon, only his eyes are huge, as are his lips and nose, and his skin is black as coal. He's wearing a little shirt that reads I LOVE WATERMELONS, and he's sitting on a pile of rinds and seeds. No pants. He's in a red diaper that looks more like a bandana.

Even *I'm* offended when I look at it.

But here's the part that's supposed to make it not racist: over the entire painting, after Eggplant X was finished, he wrote the word SHAME in big red letters, and that, according to my son, is what makes it politically correct and worth roughly eighty thousand US dollars, if you can believe that shit.

And here is the best part of this fucking story. Are you ready for it?

Eggplant X is whiter than me.

Ain't that some bullshit?

If a black artist was getting paid big coin for these sorts of shitty paintings, I'd at least feel good about him—or even *her*—having a good-paying job. Like I said before, this country fucked the blacks with slavery and we should give them first shot over more recent immigrants when it comes to making it in the land of the free. But it sure as hell didn't sit right with me that some white asshole, who goes around making other white people feel ignorant and ashamed about race relations, should make a shitload of money by painting what he himself labels racist. But this bullshit is high art, according to my son.

"It's . . . *interesting*," Sue said, just to be polite. "Why does he call himself Eggplant X?"

"He refuses to explain," Hank said. "Which I think is a smart move."

"Why?" Sue asked.

"You want to tell her, Ella?" Hank said.

"What?" Ella said.

"What sells art?" Hank asked his daughter, trying to get her to do a trick like a trained poodle.

"Stories," Ella said dutifully.

"That's right," Hank said in his college-professor voice. "People don't buy paintings. They buy stories. And everyone has a theory about Eggplant X's name."

"What's *your* theory?" Sue asked Hank.

Hank was pleased with Sue's question, because it gave him the chance to do some more art-talk jerking off, and so he said, "I think he wants you to make up your own story, which is smart. And why he's my top-selling client too. He doesn't explain any of his pieces. He says they exist free and clear of him. Once he lets them go into the world, he lets each piece take on a life of its own."

"I bet he cashes the fucking paychecks, though," I said.

"First. Please watch your language around your granddaughter," Hank shot back at me, as if he never said the word *fuck* himself. "And second, why *wouldn't* he cash those checks? It would be *un-American* to refuse what the market offers, right? That's capitalism. America's true religion. You taught me that, Pop."

Hank only calls me Pop when he's making fun of me. And I also knew my son was mocking me with the un-American comment and talk of capitalism, which I believe in wholeheartedly because I'm no lousy red fucking Communist. But regardless of all that, I let Hank's comments slide. I wanted Sue and my son to get together, and he had to appear confident and attractive to woo her. If I emasculated Hank in a battle of wits—and I could do that easily even with my fucked-up brain—Sue would never again be attracted to him. So I let him be alpha male for the evening, if only for the well-being of my granddaughter.

Hank went on to talk about Eggplant X's paintings related to "the Asian experience in America." Lots to do with dry cleaning and martial arts being racist, which I don't quite understand because Bruce Lee types and every Chinese dry cleaner in America have historically made big bank.

Asians are the best when it comes to martial arts and dry cleaning—every single moron in the entire world knows that. I use Asian dry cleaners exclusively. White people are shit when it comes to dry cleaning. And if I were making a kung fu movie, I'd make damn sure the lead was Asian. There is no white Bruce Lee. Period. I like some of Chuck Norris's politics, but he is the minivan to Bruce Lee's Corvette.

And yet I kept all this to myself and let my son puff out his pretty feathers and strut his stuff. He didn't have any other angle to run on women, and sometimes it's best to go with what you do adequately rather than try to attempt something beyond your skill set.

I could tell Hank was uneasy about Sue's reaction. He gets tense talking about race-related subjects in front of people of different ethnicities. I don't understand it, because he's always so fucking sure about his opinions in a room full of whites. If

Hank knew how many times I said the word *gook* in front of Sue, he would have had a heart attack right there and then.

There was no dessert, because Hank was trying to keep me "heart healthy," and I don't count cut-up fruit as dessert. So I said, "Someone has a bedtime that expired a long time ago," meaning *Ella, get your ass to bed* NOW. I volunteered to tuck her in so that Hank and Sue could be alone and hopefully get down to business.

Ella managed to milk more time out of her father by being cute and telling stories about how she was learning about Chile, "one of the skinniest countries in the world," which prompted me to ask Hank if Chile was a "heart-healthy country" being that it was so skinny, a good joke that he ignored completely. Because he is weak when it comes to raising a child, Ella's stall tactics worked for a good fifteen minutes, but eventually I got her to give Hank and Sue kisses on the cheeks, and then I was in the upstairs bathroom with Ella, making sure she washed her face and brushed her teeth.

This next bit of information might shock you, but I actually combed Ella's hair. Her mother wasn't there anymore to do it, and Ella had only just met Sue—and, truth be told, I like combing hair. I find it soothing. I used to comb Jessica's hair when she was depressed. Her mother used to do it for her when Jessica was little. She'd get dangerously sad back then too, especially in the winter, when there was less sun. It was in her genes. Whenever my wife started to slide south, you could see it in her hair, which would get greasy and matted-looking. I couldn't stand seeing that, and because I didn't know how to cure depression, I started combing hair. It was something

I could do. And combing Ella's hair was also something I could do.

Don't tell anyone about this shit. Both about my dead wife's depression and the fact that I like combing my granddaughter's hair. The first part is none of anyone's goddamn business, and the latter might give people the wrong idea about me. I'm not a fucking pervert or anything like that. A little girl needed her hair combed, and so I did it. Period. If Femke hadn't abandoned her own flesh and blood, it wouldn't have been necessary for me to step up, but that Dutch whore left, and I do what needs to be done.

While I was combing out Ella's long brown hair, holding the roots, making sure not to hurt her, I said, "Do you think that Ms. Sue would make a good mother?"

"I like her," Ella said. "She isn't a mommy?"

"No," I said. Then, just to test the water, I added, "She would probably love to have a kid around to take care of. You know of any little girls who need a mother?"

Ella thought about it for a few seconds and then said, "Will Ms. Sue be coming back here?"

I told her I sure hoped so.

Then Ella asked if Sue was my friend, and I said Sue was maybe my *best* friend lately, but more like a daughter.

Ella spun around here and said, "I know you hate my mother, and I'm mad at her for leaving Daddy. But I miss her. *I really miss her!*"

There were tears in her little brown eyes, and I thought up a million and one ways to kill Ella's Dutch bitch mother, but I had to push all that deep down inside of me because Ella was sobbing into my chest. Her little forehead was pushing the dog tags into my breastplate and it hurt, but I didn't say anything about that or even move Ella's head. I just put my arms around her until she cried herself to sleep, at which point I tucked her in and then tiptoed out of her room, shutting off the lights and closing the door behind me.

I went into stealth mode here and crept down the stairs just enough to get a view of Sue and Hank, who were now on the couch.

Sue kept touching Hank's forearm as they talked, which could only mean one of two things. Either she thought Hank was a homosexual—I could honestly understand why, the way he went on about art all night and insisted on being called "Henri"—or she was actually starting to fall for him.

When a non-lesbian woman reaches out and touches a non-homo man on the arm more than once in a sixty-second interval, that means she is considering doing the nasty with the man. Any half-wit with a working pecker knows that. And so I smiled. I could hear them talking—mostly about me, their only common interest.

Hank was doing bad impressions of me, exaggerating my mannerisms, voice, and conservative political opinions, making me out to be some crazy right-wing buffoon. Always easy to pick on veterans when no one is invading your country. But when the Taliban infiltrates Philadelphia, Hank will be the first to come crying to his military-trained father for help.

Normally I would have gone down there and kicked his ass for displaying his ignorance in such a cavalier manner, but I had a little girl in need upstairs. That was the mission now.

And Sue was smiling, which at the time seemed to indicate that I was winning, no matter what the fuck Hank thought.

I was just about to go to bed when my son asked Sue why she hung out with me. He asked the question in a way that implied he couldn't believe *anyone* would willingly spend time with his old man.

Sue laughed and said she enjoyed my company.

Then Hank asked why, saying the word *why* like Sue had claimed she liked having her toenails pulled out with pliers.

"Don't you ever feel like everyone is bullshitting you?" Sue said. "Just saying what they think you want to hear? Like everyone is constantly lying, and we never really know a single person at all? I don't feel like that when I'm around your father. I might not always agree with his point of view, but I'm always certain I at least know it."

Sue gave Hank a chance to respond here, but he didn't take it. "You'll miss him when he's gone," she said.

"Didn't he tell you?" Hank said. "He's not buying the bullet. He's going to live forever!"

Sue said again that Hank would miss me when I was gone.

For some reason, Hank got nostalgic here and started talking about this great day we had all spent together as a family in the Poconos—Hank, Jessica, my parents, and me. I'll tell you about that day later on. I don't want to talk about it right now. But as Hank described it to Sue in vivid detail, I knew there was a part of him deep down that still loved his father, and that made the girly-man tears want to start leaking from my eyes.

So I went back upstairs and lay myself down in the guest room. The brain meds had me feeling like someone had squirted crazy glue on my eyelids. I was snoring in no time at all.

When I woke up the next morning, I checked Hank's bedroom, hoping to find a little yellow woman in bed with him, but no such luck. Honestly, I would have been a smidge disappointed if Sue had played hide-the-egg-roll with my son on the first date, because that would make her a little slutty, giving it up so easily, especially considering the fact that he didn't really have much game when it came to women. Sue wasn't the type of broad who would be easily impressed by Hank's money or his art-dealer lifestyle or his fucking hybrid car that he plugs in every night like a pussy.

Women are highly influenced by their fathers, who become their default standards for a decent man. Sue's father, Alan, was a top-tier man—battle-tested by the nastiest little yellow bastards on the planet. My son would have his work cut out for him if he wanted to impress Sue.

I met Femke's father once. Now *that* man's mother cut off his nuts at birth and then handed them over to Femke's mother when they got married. Probably kept them in a velvet pouch with silver tassels. I don't think he was allowed to open his mouth once during the few dinners I was forced to sit through with those foreigners. I felt bad for Mr. Turk and even worse for my son, who was too dumb to read the blueprint for his wife, seated across the table from him in the form of one incredibly crusty old Dutch cunt, aka Femke's mother.

I should have felt bad for myself who was gaining a bitch daughter-in-law preprogrammed to explode like a suicide vest, only she took off the metaphorical vest and put it on my son right before she escaped back into the crumbling economies of Europe. I saw it coming a decade away, but back then I didn't know how much I was going to love my granddaughter, who would make it impossible for me to steer clear of Femke forever.

I walked over to my sleeping son and poked him in the ribs.

"Stop!" he yelled as he tried to swat my hand away as if it were a mosquito.

It was almost six o'clock. Real men are up at five. I poked him again.

He asked what I wanted, and so I asked if he had fucked my genetically Vietnamese friend.

"What?" he said, stalling for time, so I repeated the question, saying, "After I went to bed. Did you nail Sue?"

"What time is it?" Hank asked, playing dumb.

So I said, "I don't mind if you sleep with her just as long as (a) she wants to sleep with you and (b) you don't break her heart. She's a good woman, Hank. Trust me."

Hank sat up and rubbed his eyes.

Then he said, "Are you insane, Dad? Because sometimes I seriously think you are absolutely fucking bonkers. People might think it's the brain surgery, but only the ones who never met you before they cut out part of your conservative brain, which just might have made you a little *less* racist, actually—which is also insane, because you are still the most offensive and the absolute most politically incorrect person I have ever met."

Hank's saying I was a little less racist was a good sign. It meant that he was hot for Sue, or at least that's what I thought.

So I said, "What happened last night? Tell me you didn't fuck it up. She'd make a great mother for Ella."

Like a dumb thirsty horse that can't find the giant freshwater lake whose edge sits less than a yard behind his own ass, Hank asked if I had seriously tried to set him up.

So I told him that I may have set up the pins, but he would have to knock 'em down, and then I asked if he had rolled another gutter ball or what.

Hank shook his head and laughed. "We had a good chat over wine, Dad. She's a lot of fun. I really liked her. I can see why you thought the two of us would get along."

I asked again what had happened, and he said nothing. "Something always happens," I said. "Don't bullshit me."

Then Hank went on about how they had only finished the wine and talked about all sorts of things, but mainly yours truly. Hank said that Sue really cares about me and that he was glad she was there for me when he and I weren't speaking. She had filled him in on a bunch of stuff that happened when he was ignoring his father. Then around ten she said she had to leave. She wanted to say good-bye to me, according to Hank, but he'd told her I was surely sleeping, which was accurate.

"There was one other extremely interesting thing Sue told me," Hank said, making eye contact, evaluating me. "Clayton Fire Bear. The name you kept repeating after your surgery—you knew him during the war?"

I didn't remember telling Sue that, which scared me. What the fuck else had I admitted while my brain was healing? Hank wasn't ready to hear the story, so I looked away.

"You can talk to me about the war, Dad, if you need to. I'll listen. Do you want to talk about it? Do you *need* to?"

That question caught me off guard. I had always wanted to protect Hank from the horrors of Vietnam, so instead of answering, I asked if he had at least kissed Sue good night.

Hank's face dropped for a second. Then he laughed and said, "Nope."

I shook my head. My son was never very good with women. "There aren't exactly a lot of cars on your freeway, son. I really hope you didn't blow it."

"Blow what?"

So I told him that he needed a new woman ASAP. "You can't afford to fuck around now."

He said he was still married, and that Femke was still Ella's mother.

"Being married didn't stop Femke from screwing a weatherman," I said.

Hank winced because the truth hurts. Then he said, "Can't you understand that I'm grieving?"

"You don't have time to grieve. You have a daughter to raise. She needs a mother here in America. One who will put Ella's needs first."

Hank started running his fingers through what little hair he has, like he always does when he's stressed out. Then he said, "You're right."

I couldn't believe my ears. It was the first time he had ever said that I was correct about anything since he was three feet tall.

"And I have a father to get healthy too," Hank continued. "Sounds like Sue could be a fantastic ally."

I asked if I was dreaming.

Hank smiled and offered to cook me a spinach and feta omelet, and when I asked if I could have toast and butter, that request was denied.

"Heart-healthy breakfast?" I said.

"Whole-being-healthy, Dad. Body, mind, and soul. What do you say? Both of us need to work on that."

Then Hank hopped out of bed and put his arm around my shoulder. He smiled as he gave me a manly squeeze. If he had quoted the second amendment and told me I was allowed to carry a concealed weapon in his home, I wouldn't have been more surprised.

It was hard to believe this sudden good turn in Granger father-son relations was legitimate. I felt like my son was trying to trick me, and I couldn't find his angle. Hank has historically always been a complete bastard to me, I kept thinking as I watched him cook the heart-healthy omelets.

Finally, after looking at every possible angle, I concluded that there was only one logical explanation. Hank must have really fallen head-over-heels in love with Sue Wilkerson. And yours truly had brought that fantastic woman into his life. Finally, after forty-some years of bickering, Hank and I found something we could both respect: a gigantic love for a genetically Vietnamese registered Republican named Sue. Or so I thought at the time.

9.

I've heard that a man only really falls in love one time, and I believe that is true, which is why I never remarried after Jessica died. What was the point? I wasn't going to do any better than I already had. Jessica was real mashed potatoes and butter. To me the rest of the women in the world would always be the equivalent of Hank's mashed cauliflower, bland and unsatisfying. He might call it "heart healthy," but the heart knows what it fucking wants, and it's hardly ever cauliflower.

Most men, of course, never manage to marry their true loves. Some wait too long and miss the opportunity. Others think with their dicks and fuck it up by sleeping with any old floozy who will open her legs. And then there are those who miss out because they are too busy chasing other dreams at work, trying to add zeroes to their bank accounts, which is always a good idea, don't get me wrong about that, definitely add a zero whenever you can, but you have to add metaphorical zeroes to your love life too, make it grow, keep it safe and true. Believe me, I know about these things because I used to be married to the best woman in the entire world.

Pretty much everything good after I returned from the land

of little yellow bastards happened accidentally and because I had a Vietnam buddy named Roger. We used to call him Roger Dodger, because he used to drive a 1966 Dodge Charger. V8 engine. Badass. Roger Dodger was a good man who—like many of us—got really fucked up in Vietnam. Came home addicted to drugs and convinced that we were all part of some social experiment conducted by higher beings, which he liked to call Light People, at the time. Needless to say, he was pretty fucking crazy back then, always high. And when he was lifted, as the brothers say today, he'd spout his theories like he was a young Jim Jones with Kool-Aid plans for his future rainbow family in Guyana.

From his grandfather, Roger inherited some money and a little house in a run-down neighborhood. He turned said house into a drug bungalow where he did an after-school business. Basically, he allowed high school kids to party there, charging them a nominal fee to smoke weed with him, take acid, do heroin when he had it, and drink themselves silly. These were kids whose parents were both working to make ends meet, and so they were pretty much unsupervised. Roger Dodger took advantage of that.

He also had a bit of a thing for underage girls, although back in the late sixties having sex with a young woman in high school wasn't the headline-grabbing crime that it is today. Roger had another Vietnam vet living with him for a time, who I didn't like. One of the few vets that I didn't get along with. His name was Brian, and he was a real fucking piece of shit, let me tell you.

When I was with Tao in the jungle, I promised myself that

if I made it home alive, I would never ever eat another fucking snake for dinner, I would never again sleep in a tree, I'd never walk around for weeks in wet rotting boots, and I'd never take shit off of any man because I was an underling, if I could help it. Great motivation for making money here in America, let me tell you. Motivation is what enables you to do what other men will not. My competition in the banking world had never killed anyone, let alone had their mental endurance tested by the little pricks in Vietnam. When you have watched your friends die in your arms, felt the flesh rot off your feet, and gone nose to nose with pure evil, going the extra mile with an investor—laughing at his dumb jokes, having that extra late-night drink when you'd much rather be home with your family, and sniping the in-house competition by inserting the right word at the right time into the boss's ear—is like R&R in Hawaii compared to day-to-day wartime Vietnam. I used to just laugh when my fellow bankers complained about their imaginary stress. I was the apex predator in any jungle or boardroom, and I made sure everyone was damn sure aware of that fact. Since I was bringing in big-time money, my superiors looked the other way whenever some pussy colleague complained about me. People in power take care of the apex predator. Always. Doesn't matter if we are wearing suits or camouflage. The rules are the same.

When I returned home, after some crazy time in a military loony bin in Kansas, which I'll talk about later, I used the GI Bill to take the Temple challenge, which meant that I enrolled at Temple University in Philadelphia. Previously, I had been thinking I would be an engineer, but I ended up studying business and economics, which, it turns out, is a lot like war. Like I just said, if you are smarter and tougher and more ruthless than everyone else, you can win the money game and usually do. So I wasn't getting stoned and drunk back then. I was studying my ass off and working two jobs, one at a bank and another as a carpenter on the weekends.

Even still, I tried to keep in touch with my Vietnam veteran friends, if only to check up on them and try to encourage them to make something of whatever life they had left, which was a lot harder than it sounds to people who have never been to war in some shithole country.

The vets of today coming back from Afghanistan and Iraq have it pretty fucking bad, and many who would have been killed in Vietnam come home maimed these days because of advancements in medicine, which means worse rehab and harder handicapped lives. But I'd still say that coming home a veteran in the sixties was much, much worse than coming home a veteran now. We honor the troops everywhere these days with ribbons and patriotic beer commercials and hometown hero announcements at sporting events where they put veterans in uniforms up on the big screens and everyone claps. All good. Better than being spit on. But I don't mean to say it's easy coming home from war today, because it fucking isn't. Not by a long shot.

Back in the late sixties, whenever I stopped by Roger Dodger's, there were at least a dozen teenage girls high out of their little minds. Some of these girls were only fourteen or fifteen. A lot of guys got a taste for that in the whorehouses in Vietnam. I knew that wasn't good stateside. I didn't want to tell my friends what they could or couldn't do, but these girls had never left suburbia and therefore had no idea what killers they were partying with. I'm not saying that all Vietnam veterans were dangerous when they came home, but Roger and Brian were definitely taking advantage of these underage girls, impressing them with war stories and then getting them high so that they could get laid on a regular basis, all while taking money off them too. And the girls didn't know that they were playing with live rounds, sticking loaded guns in their mouths, and other orifices too. I was on a hair trigger myself, but at least I was sober most days. Drugs can be calming, but sometimes they aren't.

I'd have a beer with Roger when all these kids were there, and I'd say, "What the fuck are you doing, man?"

He'd laugh and say, "I'm enjoying the fruits of America!"

I'd try to talk to him about the GI Bill and maybe having a future, but his setup was too good. All the drugs he wanted, a free place to live, and an inexhaustible supply of teenage poontang gyrating to the Doors or the Stones or whatever the fuck else we were listening to back then.

I'd been to Roger's place dozens of times without having to fight anyone, back before I met Jessica, so the following story doesn't represent a typical day in the civilian life of David Granger.

It was a Saturday in the dead of winter. Too much snow on the ground for carpentry work. I had the day off, so I went to check up on Roger and try to talk his ass into putting down the weed pipe and taking the Temple challenge, although I can't remember if they called it the Temple challenge back then.

Maybe Bill Cosby started all that later, but before we found out that he was a serial pervert in addition to being Temple's best-known alumnus. But I remember Roger's Dodge Charger was covered in several inches of ice and snow. The driveway hadn't been cleared, or the sidewalk, but there were all of these footprints frozen in the snow. All of them about the size of teenage-girl feet.

I could hear the music blasting as I approached. I remember it was "Friday on My Mind" by the Easybeats because that was a dumb fucking song to play on a Saturday, or at least that's what I thought when I was standing there freezing my ass off, waiting for someone to open the door. When no one did, I turned the knob and let myself in.

The pot smoke was so thick, it looked like the house was on fire.

"Close the fucking door!" someone yelled. "Keep the smoke in!"

I saw a few young girls completely naked and passed out on the floor, so I started looking for Roger before I got a contact high myself. I could usually get him to sit with me in the kitchen, where no one else really partied. Everywhere I looked, there were drugs and teenage flesh. I couldn't find Roger, and no one was responding to any of my questions because of the drugs and also the music was so fucking loud so I went upstairs.

At the top of the stairs I heard a young woman screaming for help, only it was hard to hear over the music, so no one was helping her. The bedroom door was locked, so I kicked it in.

Brian was standing there naked, holding a revolver with

one hand and stroking his little erect dick with the other, all while saying crude things like he was going to "widen her" and "make her evil" and other perverted ideas I won't repeat here because they are just too fucked up for the average ear. And if something is too fucked up for me to repeat, you know it is really nasty. He was so high he didn't even turn to face me.

I kept my eye on the gun, which was pointed at the floor, but could easily have been pointed at my face within seconds. I don't take chances with armed men tripping on acid and weed and alcohol and whatever else they had scored. So I simply coldcocked Brian. My right fist hit the right side of his skull, and then his face hit the floor. Only he pulled the trigger as he fell, shooting a bullet through the wood boards below him.

I quickly kicked the gun out of his hand, made sure he was out cold, and then ran downstairs to see if anyone had been shot. Miraculously, the bullet passed through without hitting any of the dozen people partying on the first floor. The music was so loud and everyone was so wasted that no one even knew that a gun had been fired. That's how fucked up these people were. With everyone out of harm's way, I went back upstairs to check on the young girl Brian had sexually assaulted.

She was crumpled up in the corner, shaking and crying. When I touched her shoulder, she jumped and then screamed, but then she threw herself at me, so I put my arms around her in an attempt to calm her down.

After a minute or so, she looked at me and said, "Who are you?"

I told her my name and asked for hers.

"Jessica," she said, and then went on to explain that she was

Roger Dodger's kid sister. I'd later learn that she had been coming around the house to try and help get her brother out of his drug haze, but instead had ended up getting sucked into the scene and participating. If you were in that house, you had pot smoke in your lungs whether you wanted it there or not.

To make a long, awful, fucked-up story short, Jessica didn't manage to get Roger to stop using drugs to escape his Vietnam memories. It was the other way around: Roger got Jessica to start smoking pot and tripping, because he believed it would help cure her depression, which, to be fair, was severe. People thought LSD cured everything back then. I never took the stuff myself; I had enough wild images in my head already. Since Roger was a consummate drug user and constantly having sex with teenagers—he loved the Catholic schoolgirl uniform—he often lost track of what his sister was doing in his house, which is how Brian got to Jessica. Put a lamb in a cage with a tiger, and there will be blood.

What I didn't know at the time was that Brian was dead. Someone finally found him, naked and ice cold, hours later. He had so many drugs in his system, it was assumed that he overdosed or simply fell down and hit his head too intensely on the hardwood floor. Brian had a wild bush of hair on his skull back then, so maybe no one saw the bruise on his temple, I don't know. Or maybe he really did overdose on drugs, and I'm just taking credit for a punch that really wasn't all that impressive. I mean, you don't exactly have to be Smokin' Joe Frazier to knock out a man who is tripping off a veritable cornucopia of drugs.

The point of this tale is that up until right now, only two

people in the world knew that I had coldcocked Brian before he died: Jessica and me. The cops never questioned me about Brian's death. I'm not sure that anyone else even remembers my being in the party house that day—they were all so fucking high. And Jessica never said anything to anyone else about my dropping Brian like the sack of shit he was.

That's all I know. Brian died. No one connected me to his death. I wasn't about to give myself up, either. I'd killed a lot of gooks in my day, and if I thought about it—which I don't—I'd probably get to feeling sadder about the little yellow bastards I offed than I would about Brian. Honestly, the local police probably also celebrated a deadbeat Vietnam veteran's death. Drugs were a great patsy scapegoat too. America hates drugs. And Brian became a poster child for just saying no in that community. Everyone was happy with that narrative. End of story.

Before you get to feeling too bad about Brian's untimely demise, allow me to prove to you that he absolutely deserved to die. You're probably already feeling squeamish about two Vietnam veterans partying with and screwing a bunch of girls in high school, right? Well, if you think that's bad, it gets even worse. Brian's fucking wasn't always consensual. That's right. Brian was a piece-of-shit rapist. A true misogynist, to use one of my son's favorite insults.

But Jessica and I didn't know Brian was dead when we left the house that day. We just thought he was knocked out, sleeping it off on the bedroom floor. Jessica asked me to get her out of that crazy place, so I put her in my 1964 GTO, and we drove around on the snowy roads, smoking cigarettes and listening to the radio.

I had been around enough fucked-up people to know that Jessica needed time to process whatever the fuck hellish ordeal happened to her in that house, and I didn't have anything else to do that day. Several times I asked her if there was anywhere she wanted to go, and she kept asking if we could just drive. Gas wasn't free, but neither was love, and some part of me knew right there and then that I had fallen hard and irreversibly. I didn't want to fuck this young girl, I wanted to help her—but I also wanted her to like me, even love me. Mostly, I wanted her to think of me as the opposite of that rapist disgrace to his country, Brian.

After hours of driving in a huge circle around Philadelphia, which took us into Delaware, Pennsylvania, and even up to Trenton, Jessica asked how I'd been able to come home from the war and do better than her brother Roger. "Do you have a secret?" she asked.

I didn't know how to answer that one. To be honest, I have often wondered why so many of my combat brothers were unable to rejoin civilian life. Some never really left the jungle. Many others never could keep a job, let alone make the sort of money I made. I wish there were a formula or a set of instructions I could give to other veterans, but the truth is, I don't really know why I didn't end up dead or burned out on drugs and alcohol. Something inside my brain switched when I was eating fucking snakes and sleeping in trees and killing gooks. *Fuck this shit*, it said. *I'm going home to the greatest country in the world, and I'm going to make something of myself. Never again will anyone make me live the way I was forced to live in the jungle. I'm going to* use *my freedom.*

I think that many Vietnam vets believed that no matter what they did, they would never have any control over their lives. Powerful, faceless men would always pull the strings, so why should the powerless non-string-pullers give a fuck? Playing the puppet while high became easier than cleaning up enough to cut strings and kill puppet masters. I understood their logic, and believe me when I say I still haven't killed all of the puppet masters, not even by a long shot. But I decided that I wanted to pull at least some of my own strings, even if I could never pull them all.

I couldn't have said as much back in the GTO, cruising around with Jessica. I might have been to Vietnam and back. I might have killed hundreds of gooks. But I was still just a kid.

I remember we were on the New Jersey Turnpike when Jessica told me she was pregnant. I've never told this story to anyone, and obviously Hank didn't know shit about this for most of his life. I wouldn't be spilling all of this now if I didn't have a good reason to do so, and if I didn't have your word that all of this will remain classified until I die. That being said, if you tell anyone about this little secret of mine before I'm in the ground, I will break into your house in the middle of the night, slit your throat while you are sleeping, and annihilate your entire family. I have your name and title—it wouldn't be all that hard to track down your home address. Believe me. Nothing personal here. Of course I trust you, or I wouldn't be telling you all of this in the first place. But it makes me feel better to let you know that there will be big-time fucking consequences if any of this shit becomes public. If you break our little agreement, you will be sorry. And dead.

Brian was the father, Jessica went on to tell me. He had raped her a month before. The day I showed up she had gone back to the house to speak with Brian about her options, but like I said before, he was high out of his mind, so all he could do in response to Jessica's pleas was jerk off. Nice guy, right? I have no regret killing that motherfucker, if it was indeed my fist that took his life. They say killing a man with one punch is one hell of a hard thing to do, so maybe it was divine intervention. If you believe in God, we may be able to agree on that.

Back in the GTO, I glanced over at Jessica. It was nighttime by then, and I could only see her face when we passed under lights, or when cars going in the opposite direction illuminated her with their headlights for a second or two, creating an eerie sort of strobe effect. I could clearly see that she was contemplating buying the bullet. She was a senior in high school. Beautiful. Radiant. And I would later learn that she was an extremely talented painter. But that night, as we drove around, she was contemplating death. I could smell the Grim Reaper there with us. Like I said before, I know that motherfucker Death better than you know yourself.

Scary fucking words started coming fast and furious out of her pretty little mouth. I knew she was closer than ever to buying the bullet, because she didn't care what I might think about her. She told me all about how Brian had coerced her into smoking too much weed, and then he used his tongue to transfer a few LSD tabs when he forced her to kiss him. I don't know too much about drugs—I'm a beer guy—but this asshole used weed and acid to make a young girl vulnerable, and then he raped her several times over the course of an afternoon. Yes, rape, because she didn't want it to happen. Period. That's rape. She was a virgin before that. And all this happened because she was genuinely concerned about her brother Roger's well-being. No good deed goes unpunished, right?

Jessica didn't want to have an abortion because she didn't think she could live with herself afterward, murdering an unborn child. She wasn't religious and was all in for women's rights. My dead wife might even have been described as a bleeding-heart liberal, if we're really being honest, but for whatever reason, she just couldn't wrap her head around killing the baby inside her—which, of course, would end up becoming Hank.

What she *could* wrap her mind around, and was working her way up to telling me about, was killing herself. That way she wouldn't have to live with the guilt of aborting her unborn child, and as an extra bonus, she wouldn't have to deal with her depression any longer either. The fact that she had been raped would go away too.

I picked up on the self-slaughter vibe way before Jessica got around to admitting that she was suicidal and so I interrupted her and told her that I had a plan that might work.

My plan was this: she and I would get to know each other over the next few weeks, and if we liked each other, we'd begin to tell everyone that I'd knocked her up, and then we'd get married. If we didn't like each other, well then, nothing was lost, and she could go ahead with her original plan.

"What original plan?" she asked me, because she hadn't yet actually admitted to being suicidal.

I told her the common Vietnam veteran theory about buying the bullet, which she hadn't heard before because her brother was too busy getting high to educate her. "If you think you're going to die, it will definitely happen. So be careful with your thoughts."

Then I told her I knew what she meant when she said she was going to just disappear, but she kept pushing me to say it. So I finally did.

"Why would you want to marry a suicidal girl?" she asked. It was a fair question. I didn't want to marry her just yet, I told her, but I liked driving around with her and thought she was pretty.

"You're attracted to the pregnant raped girl?" she said, which made me want to kill that scumbag Brian because I didn't yet know that I already had.

I told her that while she was undoubtedly feeling bad, and understandably so, she had no idea how low you can really go when it comes to feeling shitty about what you have done and what has been done to you.

"You mean about the war?" she said.

I nodded, and then for some reason I just started telling her things. Not everything I've mentioned in this here report, but things that I had never told anyone who wasn't a Vietnam veteran. I'm not quite sure why I opened up to Jessica. Maybe it's because she opened up to me. Maybe it was because she felt dirty, like I did. Maybe it was because I had dirt on her, so my sharing my dirt only made things equal. Maybe it was because she was gorgeous, because she absolutely was. After decades of thinking about all of this shit, I guess I just wanted her to feel clean by comparison. No one was dirtier than me.

Before I knew what had happened, I had talked straight through the night about my tour, and we were somehow on a beach in Sea Isle City, watching the sun come up over the ocean. There was snow on the sand, and it was fucking freezing cold, but we were wrapped up together in an old scratchy green wool army blanket I kept in the trunk. I had my arm around her, and she was leaning her head on my chest. I thought about the life inside her belly.

On the one hand, that baby had the genes of a fucking rapist. But I had been exposed to a lot of Agent Orange in Vietnam, and I was worried about my ability to father a child myself. I wasn't stupid. I knew how fucking terrible that potion was way before any civilians started talking about it on the news. I had seen firsthand what it could do to an entire living, breathing ecosystem. And I guess I wanted to atone for some of my sins too. Also, I knew that Brian hadn't seen as much jungle action as I had, so therefore he had less exposure to Agent Orange. Brian's baby probably wouldn't be as genetically fucked-up compared to a child I might biologically father.

I asked Jessica what she wanted out of life, and she said she only needed art supplies and a room to paint. That was easy enough to accomplish—I was sure I could make money. Any white man with half a brain in America can make a good living if he works hard and really wants to.

And on that beach in Sea Isle City, I decided that I was going to marry Jessica and be the father to her bastard son—only I'd never tell him he was the bastard son of a lowdown scumbag rapist, and I wouldn't let Jessica tell him either. It would be four more weeks before I shared my decision with Hank's mother, which is also when I asked for her hand in marriage. But I had made up my mind right there and then on the beach less than twenty-four hours after first meeting Jessica. When it's love, you just know.

I hadn't asked to be a killer of gooks over there in Vietnam. My government said that gook killing was what needed to be done, and so I did it to the best of my abilities. And I hadn't asked to be a father either, but there was a young woman who needed a man to step up to the plate. It was a mission that simply needed to be done. Period.

Learning about Brian's death later that night in some ways sealed the deal for me. I did the moral math in my head: without a doubt, a narrative had clearly formed. God had given me a chance to atone. And after my time in the jungle, I fucking needed it. Sometimes you just have to take what comes your way and do the absolute best you can with the opportunity.

10.

Hank and Sue's second date took place at the Philadelphia Museum of Art because my son wanted to educate my friend on the finer points of art appreciation, which, of course, is just another way of saying that Hank wanted to show off. Peacocks flaunt whatever feathers they got, and goddamn useless knowledge of art Hank had in spades.

Ella and I went along to chaperone, but I made sure we kept our distance so that we wouldn't be throwing a wet blanket over the fire we were trying to ignite.

Hank spent a lot of time yapping at Sue in the South Asian Art section, even though they didn't have shit from Vietnam. Mostly India, Nepal, Tibet, and Pakistan.

Then he spent just about a millennium talking about his boys Gustav Klimt and Egon Schiele, because he majored in those two clowns back in art appreciation school or whatever they call it. When it comes to Klimt and Schiele, Hank will talk *both* your ears off.

There's this one section called Masters of American Craft

where they basically hang rugs on the wall and call it art, except these aren't even fancy expensive Persian rugs but shitty half-finished American rugs.

I don't like Iranians one fucking bit, and Persian is just an old-fashioned word for Iranian, only your average American moron doesn't know that these days. But those Iranian motherfuckers are the best at making rugs, you have to give them that. Bomb every single one of the Ayatollah Ass-A-Hole-A's nuclear weapon–making facilities, but let them keep all the rug factories they want. A Persian rug really classes up a dining room, let me tell you. I even have one in my office because I like the way it feels on my bare feet. Heirloom quality. Never buy a rug from a non-Persian.

But back to the Masters of American Craft section of the art museum. There are these creepy dollhouses in plastic cubes and sundry bullshit that make my son cream his pants, he gets so goddamn turned on when in the presence of that dumb stuff. Sue did a good job faking enthusiasm, but Ella, having done this Hank Art Museum Tour monthly since she was born, was bored to tears. I took her to look at the suits of armor they have there, and we talked about princesses and knights while Sue and Hank were somewhere else, hopefully falling in love.

Ella and I were looking up at a fake man on a fake horse, both of which were wearing heavy armor, when I told her that one of my first dates with her grandmother had been right here at the art museum.

"Why aren't Grandmom Granger's paintings hanging up in this museum?" Ella asked, and I shrugged because my dead wife was the fucking best painter ever to breathe American air, but I couldn't tell a seven-year-old the true answer to her question.

"Was she pretty?" Ella asked, and I needed more than a gesture to answer that one, so I told Ella that her paternal grandmother was the prettiest woman who ever lived and that I fell in love with her the instant that I saw her. "One look, and I was hooked." Of course I left out the part about accidentally killing that rapist Brian. My granddaughter hopefully didn't even know what rape was. And like I said before, I vowed to tell no one about killing Brian, and I didn't until now in this tell-all report because we have a fucking deal.

But Jessica and I had gone to the art museum on our second date back in January of '69, which took place the day after we spent the night driving around in my GTO. Jessica loved going to the art museum on Sunday mornings. I think they might have let students in for free way back in the day, but I can't remember for sure.

I do remember her dragging me by the hand to show me a particular portrait painted by her hero, which I already mentioned was that Frenchman named Henri Rousseau. Jessica's high school art teacher had introduced her to Rousseau and had convinced her that his work hanging in art museums all over the world meant that anyone had a shot at making art that would be praised long after his or her death. It was obvious that her teacher thought his own art would someday be discovered and future critics would say that he was unappreciated as a lowly fucking high school art teacher, but I never said that to Jessica, because she lit up whenever she talked about this Rousseau dude.

The painting Jessica wanted me to see that Sunday morning was the one Hank mentioned to Sue during our first family dinner together. *Carnival Evening*. Jessica and I stared at that painting for so long, I could tell you anything about it from memory. My dead wife could look at any Henri Rousseau for an eternity and never be bored for a second. Also, we used to have a print of *Carnival Evening* in our living room, so I used to study it at home too, trying to figure out why Jessica and Hank thought it was so fucking world-altering—why they had chosen this painting out of all the millions that existed all over the globe as their personal *Mona Lisa*. Why hang this particular Rousseau in our house, when I would have bought them any print they wanted?

Carnival Evening depicts a costumed couple standing in front of barren skeletal trees. A full moon hangs in the top right corner. There are clouds and stars in the sky. I could never figure out if it's supposed to be sunset and the costumed couple is going to a carnival, or it's sunrise and the couple is returning home. In the bottom left corner, there's a strange structure that looks like the roof of a small house, only there are no walls underneath, so it appears to float for the most part.

Why?

Couldn't fucking tell you.

Only a single corner pillar is present—the front right—on which Rousseau painted what looks like a decapitated head, at least to me, but remember that I've seen horrific shit, so maybe I'm just projecting, as my VA therapist says.

The couple has brown skin, which, aside from the connection to his mother, is probably why Hank likes this particular painting so much. The brown-skinned couple is at the center bottom. The man wears a puffy white outfit and a pointy hat that makes him look like a cross between a clown and a magician and a Ku Klux Klan Grand Wizard, which is sort of ironic, being that he has brown skin. The woman wears a hat that looks like a beehive, a blue dress lined in orange and yellow, and a white apron.

Arm in arm, they share a concerned glance as they move out of the trees and into the cleared land—maybe like they just finished doing something dangerous in the forest. Believe me, I know *that* fucking look.

Jessica used to say shit like "The play between the moonlight in the sky and the barren forest is fantastic." To me it was just another painting in a place filled with thousands, but I was no artist. I admit that I couldn't paint anything remotely as interesting as Henri Rousseau could, but I still didn't get why Jessica loved this dude so much.

So I asked her. Turns out Henri Rousseau was a lowly toll collector for much of his adult life. Some old-time French elitists used to call him a "Sunday painter," which meant he was not a pro. They also called him a "naive painter," which basically meant the same thing, only it had the added effect of making him sound like a child. Others called what he did "primitive," which would have been racist had he not been white, albeit French.

Any fucking way, Henri Rousseau started painting the way he felt like painting, which often meant dreaming up crazy scenes that featured animals he had never encountered in real life and in jungles he had never been to.

He has this crazy painting hanging in MoMA in New York City called *The Dream*, which depicts a naked woman reclining on a couch in the middle of the jungle. A black werewolf-looking cat man plays a horn behind two female lions emerging from the leaves and flowers. I know because we had this one hanging in our house too, in the TV room. I'd stare at it whenever TV got too boring, which was often. An elephant, a snake, a monkey, and a few birds are in the foliage. This is some crazy LSD-trip shit, believe me. And everyone said so when it was first displayed, only they didn't know about LSD yet, they just thought it looked fucking insane.

Rousseau would hang his wild paintings at the big fancy French art shows, and people would openly mock him. That Spanish motherfucker Picasso even got a bunch of artists together to throw a mock party to "celebrate" Rousseau's peculiar brand of genius, and mock him they did unmercifully. All of the critics and great artists of the day thought Rousseau was a fucking bush-league hack at best and completely bonkers at worst, but he believed in what he did enough to keep going, painting his bizarre jungle scenes like a middle finger held high. Something inside his heart told him he was a genius and all of the French assholes around him were wrong, which I could understand, being that the French are almost always wrong, even about themselves.

A week or so after Jessica and I met, we went to MoMA in New York City and looked at *The Dream* for the first time, because she had always wanted to do that. She stood in front of that big-ass painting for ten years, and then she told me that when a reporter asked Henri Rousseau about *The Dream* and why he had painted a sofa in the middle of the jungle—no doubt mocking him under the guise of journalism, because all reporters are petty gossips and liars—Rousseau allegedly replied, "Because one has a right to paint one's dreams," only in French, not American English. I didn't give a shit about any of this, but I loved the way Jessica's face lit up when she was talking about art or painting or gazing at the work of her heroes.

And that's all Jessica wanted to do. Paint her dreams. I remember all this shit about Henri Rousseau because Jessica told me about the French toll collector billions of fucking times and we took countless trips to art museums all up and down the East Coast, for many of which Hank was present, so instead of facts about baseball players and comic books, he knows these art stories too.

And so while Ella and I were talking about knights and princesses in the armor section of the art museum, Hank was probably telling Sue the same shit about Henri Rousseau that I'm telling you here, not that you probably give a flying fuck about art, being that you work for the government. But you did tell me I had to tell you absolutely *everything* that has happened to me since I returned from Vietnam, especially everything related to my disabilities, and I'm trying to do my best here, condensing almost fifty fucking years into this little narrative, which is a truly heroic feat considering that your employer—Uncle Sam—cut out part of my goddamn brain not too long before all this shit went down with Sue and Hank. Fuck you a lot for that, by the way. And I am still to this day not entirely myself, so this isn't exactly easy. You already know I have never backed down from hard.

But standing there looking at the fake horse and man in armor at the art museum, holding my granddaughter's hand, talking about my dead wife, all of a sudden it felt like a lightning bolt had struck my skull. Before I knew what was happening, I was on the floor, convulsing and foaming at the mouth. I kept trying to pull myself together because I didn't want to frighten Ella, but I had no control. Zilch. It was like someone had plugged my brain into a socket and then jacked up the electricity as high as it would go. Fucking seizure.

The next thing I knew, I was in an ambulance headed back to Jefferson Hospital and all of the fucking moron doctors and cold bitch nurses within. And the Puerto Rican EMT riding next to me is saying everything is going to be okay. So I said I just wanted to go home and we didn't need to bother with the hospital. He kept trying to smooth-talk me like Puerto Ricans do, saying I just needed to undergo some routine tests, using that easy Puerto Rican way that helps to get them laid so often by women of all ancestries, but I wasn't Tony, he wasn't Maria, and this sure as hell wasn't *West Side Story*, and I told him so.

I don't think he had ever seen *West Side Story*, because he made a strange face, which was surprising, because I would think all Puerto Ricans would have seen the only musical about their struggle to integrate into American society. Maybe Puerto Ricans don't like musicals, which would explain why we haven't yet made Puerto Rico a state, because musical theater is in every true American's heart, whether they are brave enough to admit it or not.

I fucking love musicals, which is something you probably wouldn't have guessed, because most people stereotype Vietnam veterans as non-musical-theater patrons, let alone enthusiasts. But you don't have to be a homo to love musicals. That's a common fallacy, because of the fact that almost every gay loves musical theater. I go to musicals with Gay Timmy and Gay Johnny all the time. We even have a subscription together at the Forrest Theatre, but that doesn't make me gay, not even in the slightest.

Chicago is my favorite musical. I have the DVD of that one, and I watch it all the time, even though Timmy says straight men always like *Chicago* best. I don't like Richard Gere's politics because he's a pussy liberal, and fuck the Dalai Lama for not going after China more aggressively, but I have to admit Gere is pretty good in *Chicago*. Catherine Zeta-Jones and Renée Zellweger are both grade-A pieces of ass in that film, which is how you know they make musicals for non-gays too.

Anyway, I'm in the ambulance when I remembered Ella and so I asked the Puerto Rican EMT what happened to my granddaughter and he said he didn't know because he just got me on the stretcher and put me in the vehicle. That was the extent of his job description. And I almost had another heart attack right then and there, worrying about Ella, who I thought must have been scared to death watching me convulsing on the floor. Thank God I wasn't driving this time.

But thank God twice because—along with Sue and Hank—Ella was there at the hospital shortly after I arrived, which made me happy because it meant my granddaughter was okay, but sad because my seizure had fucked up Sue and Hank's second date. No one falls in love at a goddamn hospital, that's for sure.

We had to wait a long time for a room to open up, and then even longer for the bullshit tests because hospitals are run even more inefficiently than the Obama White House. I also had to stay overnight because the doctors who needed to read the test results were on some faraway mountain skiing. They had all made so much fucking dough off my brain surgery, super rich people don't work on Sundays, and there's always fresh powder in the world somewhere.

They all came back in on Monday with huge grins on their thieving faces and fantastic tans—white masks where their ski goggles had been—to read my test results and determine I needed an adjustment in my meds, which they themselves had originally prescribed, by the way, but do you think they apologized for giving me a combination of pills that made me feel like I was taking a ride in the electric chair? Hell no. The yahoos just gave me a different combination of pills and told me to trust them, which I had to do, because the alternative was death, or so they said. And I pay for my own health care too, so this is the best available in the land of the free. I'd have been dead long ago if I were relying on the fucking VA hospitals.

The next day Ella was in school and Sue was at work, so it was just me and my boy. Because he doesn't know shit about medicine or how powerful men operate, Hank kissed all of the doctors' asses unabashedly. It was pitiful. Powerful men never respect the ass kissers, they only respect power, but my son had somehow made a good living smooching the sphincters of rich people, so he wasn't about to listen to his old man when it came to dealing with arrogant skiers who sometimes practiced medicine whenever the snow melted or they got tired of the slopes. I knew Hank had written off my opinions long ago, and so I saved my breath.

And then, *finally*, my pitiful trip to the rob-you-while-you-are-sick hospital was over, and Hank and I were driving back to his home. I asked to stop at my own house, thinking I'd like to pick up some more weapons, but my request was denied.

"Thought we were going to lose you there," Hank said as he drove his tree-saving plug-in car made by little rice-eating men in some godforsaken faraway land.

"Only the good die young," I told him. "Can't get rid of me that easily."

I said I was sorry to have ruined his second date, which made him laugh for some reason.

Then Hank said, "Did you check your ankle holster lately?"

I had completely forgotten that I was packing heat at the art museum. I reached down for my ankle and felt nothing. "Where the fuck's my Glock?"

He told me that Sue had taken it home for me, and I wouldn't be needing it anymore. And then he went on and on about how he didn't want any guns in his house. Not around Ella. "*None!*" he kept saying. My son was apparently letting the first offense slide "on account of" and "only because of" my brain surgery. However, I would get "no more strikes." Then he said, "Are we on the same page here?"

"Sue took my gun?" I said, because at least she was trained by her father on how to handle firearms. I had tried to train Hank, but he flat-out refused to fire a weapon, even when he was a boy.

A month before Jessica died, she dumped all of my guns and

ammo into a bathtub full of water in an attempt to destroy my entire collection. I wish to God I could take back the things I said when I found out what she had done. I don't know why I'm thinking about this right now, but my screaming at Jessica in the bathroom is one of the worst memories I have, including the horror show year I spent in Vietnam. I was a fucking monster that night. I didn't hit her, but I smashed the mirror with my bare fists, bloodying my knuckles, which upset my wife even more. Jessica shouldn't have done what she did, but she wasn't in her right mind, and I loved her too much to face that truth. I didn't want the doctors to lock her away in some insane asylum, and so I tried to do my best, which wasn't good enough, obviously.

While he drove us home from the hospital, Hank kept saying, "No guns in my home. Are we clear on this issue?"

When I didn't answer, he went on and on about all sorts of bullshit handgun statistics made up by liberals who had never even touched a gun, let alone taken care of one. Then my boy actually made a legitimate point about how someone could have taken my gun off me while I was having a seizure, before Sue got to it first. Sue knew that I always carried, so she was able to discreetly remove the Glock from my ankle holster before the Puerto Rican EMT took me away. There were many people at the art museum that day, and on any other different day bad luck could have definitely sent a more violent type as an EMT, someone who needed a gun to do some base awful thing, and then what would have happened when impulse met opportunity? It was true that any old bad guy could have used my gun against me when I was convulsing, or worse yet they could have used it on Ella. The thought made me shiver.

I am more reliable than anyone out there when it comes to gun safety, but the fucking asshole skiers I had for doctors could not be trusted when it comes to my medication, which, at the end of the day, meant that I really couldn't trust myself. I decided that I would get Sue to carry for me when we were hanging out together in the city and would talk to her about that plan just as soon as I could.

To Hank I apologized, *not* for carrying the Glock without his permission, because he is not the fucking boss of me, but for putting his daughter in harm's way by having the seizure while armed. Obviously it was the fault of the dumbass doctors, who didn't know goddamn anything about medicine, or at least not enough to give me the proper dosages, but I could understand Hank's not giving a shit about that. His first priority was to protect Ella, and I had to agree with that logic.

And so I told him I would not carry a firearm again until I went seizure-free for four weeks, which seemed to satisfy him, because he said, "I can't believe we are actually in agreement. Pinch me."

I told him that I wasn't going to pinch him then or ever, but we were in agreement about Ella's safety coming first. Then I added, "Don't get cocky, son. I'm not dead yet. You ain't never gonna ever eclipse me, because I'm gonna live forever. And there ain't no man better than your father when it comes to completing missions and taking care of business. I'm a *real* man. You hear me?"

Hank stared through the windshield for a few minutes as we crossed the Ben Franklin Bridge. Then, as we were driving past Camden, he said, "You were telling Ella about Mom. At the art museum. She told me last night when I was tucking her in."

"Hope that's not illegal too," I said.

But Hank actually approved. I knew because he said, "Would you mind telling me about Mom's artwork again? It's the closest I'll ever get to seeing one of her finished paintings."

So I told Hank what I remembered, which was a lot actually. Jessica painted for a decade, so she managed to finish hundreds of works. I was the only one who ever saw any of them—or so I thought. She kept them hidden in her garage studio, which was always locked. At the end, she wouldn't even let *me* into her work space, because she felt that her paintings were visual representations of all that was going on in her mind. Since her mind was so fucked up with depression, she was worried about infecting others with her art, especially me, because of all that had happened to me during the war. Jessica had actually started to believe that others might become mentally ill simply by looking at her artworks.

But I didn't tell Hank about those later years; I told him about the beginning, when Jessica was still a teenager, painting more hopeful pieces at the start of our marriage. The boy spent many days and nights in a basket next to her easel. Sometimes I'd come home from work and find different-colored blobs of paint on his clothes, arms, legs, and face. My son loved when I talked about that. Without interrupting, adult Hank listened to me go on and on about his mother, and when we pulled into his driveway, I caught him wiping a tear off his cheek. I didn't call him on that girly-man behavior because sometimes I also feel like shedding a tear or two when I think about a nineteen-year-old Jessica looking up from a canvas big as her, smiling at me with paint smudges all over her face, like camouflage. Her long, brown hair is always braided into pigtails, and she is perpetually in overalls, as if she were a farmer riding on a tractor. All she needed was a piece of hay hanging out of her mouth. You could see the light in her eyes back then. It was bright as goddamn June moonbeams shimmering off ocean waves still warm from the day's sun.

11.

By now you probably have pieced together why I might be so immediately sympathetic toward a rape survivor like my dead wife Jessica. You have access to my secret military records, and I know you've already been through all of those, so don't even try to bullshit me about that. But since I don't have access to those files at this point in time and therefore have no idea just what the fuck they say, I figure I better set the record straight about my being sexually assaulted myself.

When they shipped me home from Vietnam, they allowed me to see my parents for a weekend before I had to go to Kansas, where I was supposed to undergo a psychiatric evaluation. Like I said before, after so many days in combat, everyone becomes legally insane, regardless of his—or unfortunately *her*, these days—mental fortitude going into war. This is a well-known fact that even the liars in Washington would never publicly dispute, even if they will never send their own sons and daughters to fight wars. So fuck them. And yes, I was definitely pretty fucked in the head when I came home, but I managed to keep it together for the forty-eight hours I spent with my mother and father, eating my mother's food and smoking my father's cigarettes. Because my father had been to war, he knew I was acting, but he played along for the sake of my mother. I tried to protect her from that the best I could. If she were still alive, I wouldn't be telling you half of what I am here, but my mother died years ago without knowing these things. Mission accomplished there.

I started to really lose it on the bus ride to Kansas. I kept seeing gooks in the trees we passed and in the backseats of vehicles next to us on the highway and peeking out of gas station windows. The pajama wearers were everywhere. There was part of my mind that knew I was hallucinating, but a larger part of my mind kept saying, *Just because you are in America doesn't mean you're safe. Your government fucked you so many times overseas, what makes you think they'll stop now that you're home and within arm's reach?* Part of me—the part that was seeing little yellow bastards in American trees—was completely paranoid, I admit, but another part of me was right about a lot of things too.

I was also afraid of seeing my nemesis, that Indian, Clayton Fire Bear, on the base. He and I had arrived in Vietnam at the same time, and therefore we were set to return stateside at the same time too.

It was a long thirty or so hours on the bus, and I mostly sweated profusely and smoked Marlboro Reds. Everyone else on the bus was twitchy too. There were some guys who tried to make jokes at first, just to keep things light, but they didn't find a large enough audience, I guess, because the jokes stopped an hour into the drive.

My orders were to report to Fort Riley, which is exactly

what I did. When we finally drove onto the base, my worst fear came true. My veins became thick with adrenaline. My heart nearly exploded. That tall-ass Fire Bear was off in the distance, smoking a cigarette and just staring at our bus, waiting for us to exit. Before I could get a really good look or figure out what the fuck to do, I was thrown onto a smaller bus with a bunch of guys who looked even more jungle than me, and we were taken to another place that was more like a hospital. Just as soon as I arrived, I understood that this was where all of the *really* insane vets got sent. It was a total loony bin, with guys staring at the walls and drooling and pacing and shaking uncontrollably for no reason at all except for the nightmares playing on the insides of their skulls. Walking into that secret medical facility was a real wake-up call. I wanted out just as soon as I was in, and I made that perfectly clear, so much that they had to restrain me the first night. That took four big black guys. Maybe even five, but they hit me with a chemical restraint, and then it was lights out.

When I woke up, I immediately realized my mistake. When I met with one of the headshrinkers that day in his office, I let him know that I had decided to make something of my life—that I wanted to study business and I didn't want any more drugs in my system. All I needed was my honorable discharge, I told him, and I'd be on my way.

The shrink in charge of my file was an older man who had served in World War II, so I told him about my father, and that seemed to hold weight with him. I remember he gave me a cigar. It was almost impossible to get cigars in Vietnam, so this was a big treat, and this old man knew it too. As we sat in his office, smoking the cigars, he got me to tell him about my adventures in Vietnam, which eventually led to my talking about Tao.

Over the course of several meetings and dozens of cigars, there was much debate over whether Tao was real or my mind had invented him as a sort of alter ego, like I said before. My military shrink tried to convince me that I wanted a partner in crime, someone to share the blame for all I had done in the jungle. He argued that Tao was an innocent whose homeland had been invaded and whose family had been raped and killed. Tao had a legitimate and concrete reason for killing Vietcong, unlike me whose government sent him halfway around the world and then said kill the yellow faces just because. The old shrink, whose name I can't recall now, was very convincing. He seemed to like me and my future plans to take the Temple challenge and make a lot of money, like all good Americans should.

In spite of that first night when the brothers had to restrain me, it was obvious that I was by far the sanest man in this little secret hospital. Everyone knew it. The staff even let me outside at night to smoke cigarettes with them under the stars, which they never would have done if they thought I was crazy as all the rest.

On my last night in that place, I woke up, and there was this other absolutely fucking nuts Vietnam veteran sucking my dick. At first I thought I was dreaming and tried to wake myself up, but then I realized I was truly awake.

"What the fuck are you doing?" I screamed, and then kneed that motherfucker in the stomach hard, knocking him to the ground. He came at me again with his mouth open, so I leaped out of bed and beat the shit out of him. Once I had him on the floor, I just kept pounding away on his face. I couldn't stop if I wanted to. Instinct took over, and I did what I was trained to do by my government. It must have taken fifteen orderlies to get me off that crazy dick-sucking motherfucker, but not before I had blinded him in both eyes.

Since it was self-defense and I was a sexual assault victim and only members of the military would be able to truly understand all of this objectively, the old man who was in charge of my file moved swiftly and had me tried in a military court of law. He testified on my behalf. I was convicted and ordered to pay a two-dollar fine. They gave me two cartons of cigarettes and sent me on my way with an honorable discharge. The old shrink said he pushed for me to be tried in a military court ASAP because, once convicted, I could never be tried in a civilian court for the same crime. I realized he had done me a solid and thanked him for it.

I sometimes feel bad about blinding one of my fellow veteran brothers. He didn't choose to sexually assault me. War had driven him out of his mind, robbing him of the ability to make healthy choices. He was like a drunk stumbling around barefoot in the desert. But rattlesnakes don't give a shit if you're blackout drunk when you step on them—they just strike and pump your ankle full of venom. And horrific violence also happens when you try to suck a sleeping combat-tested US veteran's dick. Like I said before, I had been trained to terminate anything that woke me up in the middle of the night, even when it wasn't related to my dick being sucked by another man. So it was what it was.

I never told anyone about this shit before, of course, but I would think about what happened from time to time, even though—as you might imagine—I tried to avoid thinking about it as much as humanly possible. But I have sometimes also wondered if this was why I was so quick to coldcock Brian, and also why I fell for Jessica so hard at first sight.

I don't even know the name of the man I blinded. I wonder if he ever regained his sanity and made it out of the loony bin. Did they even tell him my name? Would he have been sane enough to remember what happened? Would he come after me?

This is why whenever I see a blind man about my age walking around tapping the right and left sides of a sidewalk with one of those long, thin sticks, I have a panic attack. First time that happened, I thought my heart had stopped. That blind-man tapping noise triggers all sorts of uncomfortable feelings that I've never been able to articulate proficiently. Regardless of all that, I thought I would just put this unfortunate story in here now. It's probably already in one of your secret files, so it may have been the pink elephant in our metaphorical room or whatever the fuck you want to call this here report.

I checked with my lawyers, who assure me there is absolutely no way anyone—not even the government—could press charges against me now. It was self-defense anyway, and any man on a jury would be on my side. Even gays would be horrified to wake up that way, so this isn't about being anti-homo, which I am not anyway. The man who sexually assaulted me was crazy, not gay. Needless to say, this was not a fun conversation to have with civilian lawyers. But make no mistake about it, I was the victim that morning, and if you prematurely tell anyone about this sensitive information, for obvious reasons, I will gut you like a pig and wipe your entire fucking family off the face of the earth. Nothing personal, but it's easier to trust people like you when you're scared shitless.

12.

A few days or so after my postoperation seizure, Gay Timmy gave me a call on my cell phone. He left this long message chewing my ass out for missing my personal training session. I was supposed to ease back into my workouts, and Timmy had taken the time to construct the perfect plan, which required that I missed absolutely zero sessions. He had also given me one of his most sought-after time slots, a gesture not lost on me. Everyone wanted the 4:30 p.m., but he reserved it for my sorry ass, because we're tight.

But with everything that happened, I had forgotten all about my session and missed it. No excuses—that slipup was on me, and I had to man up about it, which I absolutely did. Lucky for me, I'd had a bona fide seizure and the hospital bills to prove it, or that would have been it for yours truly working out with Timmy. He has a million and one people waiting to take your place and get rock-hard, Navy SEAL fit.

When I heard the message on my phone, I knew I had to call back quickly. I was pretty sure Timmy would forgive me for having the seizure, but I wasn't so sure about the fact that I had not canceled my appointment. I got his voice mail, which was good, because I could explain everything without his chewing out my ass again.

Like I also told you before, Timmy and Johnny were always having me over for dinner parties. I didn't much care for gay dinner parties, but I appreciated being included. To pay them back, I would pick up the bill whenever we had dinner out on musical theater nights. And I would also take them to the Union League every now and then, even though gays raise eyebrows among my conservative Republican friends there. But fuck those bigoted people. I'd go to war with Timmy and Johnny any day of the year. Even on gay pride day when they wear rainbows all over their bodies, which is not good camouflage, to say the least.

But I still got the sense that my favorite gay couple was a little insulted about my never having them to my place for dinner. I didn't mind having gays in my home one bit, only I could not cook gay food. But Hank *always* cooked gay food, and so I had a eureka moment while I was leaving the message for Timmy. After I told him all about my seizure in the art museum and meeting a rare Puerto Rican who didn't know what the fuck *West Side Story* was, I explained that my son, Hank, cooked like a gay man, and therefore I was absolutely sure they would enjoy having dinner with me at Hank's house. Then I invited them over for that Saturday night.

I also invited Sue, for all of the reasons I already stated, and because she was friends with Timmy already. If my son proved to be an inadequate host of gays, Sue could help me pick up the slack, being that—like me—she was well versed in gay friendship.

When Timmy called me back, he was concerned about my health. Like I already told you, the gays are very considerate, which is why they make fantastic buddies. Once Timmy heard that my meds had been adjusted and that I would be able to start doing a light workout within a week or so—and therefore I hadn't reneged on my commitment to fitness—he was appeased enough to talk about dinner.

I told him not to expect much because my son was heterosexual and therefore handicapped when it came to throwing dinner parties, but I sure would like to pay my favorite gay couple back for all the times they had me over, and I knew that my living with Hank was probably our absolute best shot.

Timmy laughed like he always does when I talk about homo-hetero relations. I realize that I don't know all the proper homo terms, which is why he's always laughing at me, but he also knows me for who I am and we have been through a lot, so terminology doesn't really matter so much, despite what your average liberal will tell you.

At the club I also sometimes play pickup basketball with the brothers, and they all call me honky or cracker or old man whitey or even sometimes G.I. Joe, because they like me and I even got better jobs for some of them. I used my old contacts in the city to help the blacks make some more coin, which is the best sort of reparations there is—the ability to make your own money with your own brain and your own efforts, fair and square. It has been my experience that a black will be much more appreciative than a white when it comes to help getting jobs, and that's why I stopped helping most whites, who, truth be told, far too often act like assholes.

I should probably mention that these are all high-class brothers who can afford to pay the fitness club fees. But they call each other racist names on the court—even the biggest no-no word there is, the one that not even I will say anymore—just like the black soldiers did when I was in Vietnam.

If he were ever in the gym when these guys got to shooting off their mouths, my son would immediately lecture them on which words they were and weren't supposed to use, which would get his ass beat quick and ensure that the blacks would never pick him up on a side when it came to playing basketball. He'd be standing against the wall just holding his little white pecker from then on.

But the brothers always let me play hoops, and they laugh when I call them dark meat. They even kick one of their own off the court when I walk in, just so I can run a little ball. I never last too long, so don't go feeling too bad for the dude who has to sit down.

Needless to say I am the shittiest basketball player in the gym, especially compared to these black guys who are half my age, but they respect veterans and sometimes they even let me get a shot off. I know every single one of them can jump over fucking skyscrapers, so I only get shots off when they let me. They don't make it too obvious, and everyone on both sides—all of the brothers—whoop it up for me when one of my shots eventually tickles the twine because it usually takes me five or six tries, during which they yell words of encouragement.

Sometimes I even grab some chicken wings with these guys afterward at this local bar they frequent. Only I shouldn't eat too many chicken wings on account of my shitty health, and

Timmy has a heart attack himself whenever he finds out I've been eating chicken with the brothers. It's his job to keep me healthy, and white people get extremely fat when we eat fried chicken slathered in hot sauce and blue cheese. I always argue, saying I eat the celery they serve with the wings too, but Timmy doesn't give a shit about that.

My son gets real touchy when I talk about these basketball players. Hank is afraid of black people, although he will never admit it. I'm not afraid of anyone. And that's mostly why I am down with the brothers, who even teach me their secret handshakes, which means I am almost an honorary black myself, no matter what the fuck my son says.

On the night of our homo-hetero rainbow dinner party, I combed Ella's hair and told her that my friends Timmy and Johnny would surely notice how her hair was styled and so we had better pick carefully. Ella asked for a French braid, but I have already told you how I feel about the French, and so we went with traditional American pigtails, which was Ella's second choice. Hank had gone all in for the dinner party, even though I didn't tell him we would be having gay guests. He even cooked a small amount of meat, albeit tuna, which he seared for an Asian salad, no doubt thinking of Sue's preferences.

He had purchased a new outfit too—some jeans that cost more than your car and a sweater that looked like you could not throw it in the washing machine but had to send it to a good trustworthy Asian dry cleaner. And he had styled his hair with gel so that he looked like a homo sailor from the fifties. It made me smile because it was exactly how Johnny and Timmy styled their hair, so I knew they would be impressed with my son's effort, even though he was almost bald.

I was hoping that the new fancy outfit was for Sue, who hadn't been by in some time and hadn't talked to Hank on the phone either. I know, because I watched my son put in his cell phone code one night, and then I started checking his in- and outgoing calls when he wasn't looking. On his phone I could also check his e-mail—which was mostly art-world business bullshit I will never understand—and it was clear that Hank and Sue had not been in contact. I wondered if my seizure at the art museum had fucked up everything.

One alarming bit of news my domestic espionage turned up was the fact that Hank had been talking to Femke nightly after my meds knocked my ass out for the day, which was strange, because that would be the middle of the night for Femke, who—according to my understanding at that moment—was on Amsterdam time, so two a.m. and sometimes even later for her. There was a story there, and I knew it couldn't be good for any American patriot anywhere, but I also knew I'd catch hell if Hank found out I was spying on him via his phone, so I couldn't say shit to him about it. Every night I would try to stay awake so that I could catch him red-handed, but the army of pills in my system would win out and overtake my consciousness around nine p.m. like clockwork. I was out cold a half hour later.

Me, myself, I was wearing nothing but camouflage those days. I feel safest in my lucky army-issued outfit, and I had been through a lot in a short amount of time at that juncture. My friends all understood and didn't say anything about my dressing like a soldier. The black dudes at the fitness club sometimes wore camouflage too, which was another reason we got along, even though they had never been in the military. But I shined up my combat boots for that dinner party. That was my contribution to the night's ambience. I also groomed my beard and used the brand-new nose-and-ear hair trimmer Hank had discreetly left on the guest-room dresser. I'm not a moron. I got that fucking hint.

My friends all took the train into Jersey from the city, so they arrived en masse. As soon as they were in Hank's house, Timmy and Johnny began to freak out.

"Oh. My. God," Johnny said, pointing at my son's racist painting.

"Is that an original Eggplant X?" Timmy said.

The ends of Hank's proud smile almost knocked his ears clear off his head as he told them all about his business relationship with his top-selling artist. It was a lucky night for Hank, because within five minutes of meeting my friends he had all but sold one of Eggplant X's works in progress. Hank didn't even know Timmy and Johnny's names yet, but that didn't stop him from inviting them both to Eggplant X's forthcoming showing, which made them literally jump up and down. By the way they dressed and the twenty-thousand-dollar-plus matching Patek Philippe watches they each wore on their left wrists like gay wedding bands—I think they call them commitment watches or some such gay terminology, but I'm not sure—it was easy to see that Timmy and Johnny had a shit-ton of money.

Hank loves money just like everyone else, and I appreciate

that about my son because love of money is American, but I hadn't scheduled this dinner party to make Hank's pockets fatter. So I said, "These are my very best *gay* friends, Johnny and Timmy. And this is my only son, Hank."

"You don't have to announce the fact that they're gay, Dad," Hank fired at me in this bitchy way that Johnny and Timmy picked up on immediately.

"Why?" Johnny said. "It's not an insult, last time I checked."

Hank's face became the eggplant in the room, he was so embarrassed to have made a faux pas. I felt a little bad for him. Like I said before, the gays are a lot like cobras, and Johnny had definitely flared his hood at my son's attempt to embarrass me. I appreciated Johnny's getting my back, even though I didn't need any help when it came to putting Hank in his place.

In an effort to deescalate the situation, I said, "Hank's real name is Henri. I call him Hank, but he prefers Henri."

Johnny and Timmy nodded, and an astonished Hank said, "Wow."

"Why wow?" Timmy said.

"My father has never once introduced me as Henri," Hank said.

"His mother named him, but she's dead," I said.

"Where's Ella?" Sue asked. Once she learned that my granddaughter was in her bedroom, my best friend was up the stairs like a mother hen to round up her chick.

"These are for you," Johnny said, extending a fancy bag full of wine to Hank.

Hank looked inside and said, "These are fantastic bottles. Thank you," which probably meant everyone but me would be drinking wine that cost at least two hundred dollars a pop, because Hank wouldn't have been impressed if it had been anything under that.

"If we're going to ingest the calories, we're going to make them count," Timmy said. That got a good laugh, but I knew from experience that he wouldn't take more than three sips of his wine all night, which is another reason his abs are like six little stones arranged two-by-two on a slab of marble.

Johnny and Timmy insisted on helping Hank in the kitchen, and I sat back and watched as they made everything a little bit better, reorganizing the flowers on the table, spacing the silverware out a bit more, and doing something to Hank's hair at one point, which made me smile for Hank, because a bleeding-heart liberal having a legitimate gay man mess with his hair is like a Catholic being blessed by the pope. Everything falls into a nice rhythm whenever Johnny and Timmy are around. The key is, you just have to let them be in control of most things, and so I always do.

Hank asked them a million questions about how they knew me, and his jaw fell lower and lower with each one of their responses. "I had no idea that you have a subscription to the Forrest Theatre, Dad," Hank said at one point. I asked him why he didn't ever believe me when I said he didn't know shit about his father.

Sue and Ella came down the stairs, both dressed as princesses. Sue was wearing a tiara and holding a magic wand, whereas Ella had on her princess dress. Her hair was in the French braid she had asked for earlier, but I decided to let that slide too, because it looked pretty good, and Sue had undoubtedly worked really hard to get my granddaughter's hair the way she originally wanted it. The French make everything too complicated, little girls' hairstyles were no exception.

Timmy and Johnny made a big deal about everything related to Ella. A lot of dumb morons think we should keep homosexuals away from our children, but that's only because they have never seen the gays in action around kids. Johnny and Timmy have unlimited amounts of energy when it comes to talking about princesses and hairstyles and dresses and all of the other shit that Ella likes.

While my friends were talking to my princess granddaughter, I snuck outside for a cigarette, and Hank followed me. I lit up, and he didn't say anything at first. Then he said, "Dad, I feel like I don't even know you."

"Get to know me," I said. "I'm not going anywhere."

Hank gave me a confused look. I was worried that he was going to turn on the waterworks again, but instead he put his arm around me.

"Why didn't you ever mention Timmy and Johnny before?" he asked.

"You never asked," I said.

Hank pointed to my cigarette and asked for a drag.

"You don't smoke," I said.

"I used to. Before Femke," he said.

I gave him a drag, even though I didn't want him to start smoking again. Cigarette smoke is not good for Ella. I never smoke around her, but I have excellent self-control, and Hank doesn't. My son blew the smoke through the air, and then he took another drag before he gave me back my Marlboro Light.

"You can talk to me about anything. I won't judge you. I'll just listen. I'm here for you, Dad." Hank said this in a way that made me believe he was actually sincere, but I didn't want to get into all that horrible shit while our perfectly nice dinner party was taking place, so I just puffed on my smoke and said nothing.

He kept his arm around me for another ten seconds or so before he gave me a squeeze and then went back inside.

Across the street an old lady was watching me through her bay window. I waved at her, but she didn't wave back. Instead, she pulled the curtain. Then I remembered I was in full camouflage, which sometimes makes nonmilitary types nervous.

As I finished my cigarette, I thought about the dinner party I had cobbled together. Hank's house had become a *true* melting pot. It was nice to have such a fantastic collection of friends inside, getting along with the only family I had left. I should have known better when it came to thinking everything was going good for me, because that's always when something shitty happens, and that night was no exception.

A cab pulled up right on cue, and that Dutch cunt Femke popped out, wearing a bright yellow coat and black leggings so that it looked like she might be naked otherwise underneath. My daughter-in-law dyes her hair vinyl-record black and keeps her bangs razorblade straight, so that they cover her eyebrows, which prevents you from knowing what mood she's in. Her skin is completely drained of color, like all the evil witches in Ella's cartoons.

I immediately pointed to the cabdriver—who was wearing

a little Muslim knitted cap, by the way—and told him not to leave.

Femke asked what I was doing there, and I told her that I had moved in because Hank needed help raising Ella, now that she had abandoned her family.

Then she called me "Aap" again and tried to push her way around me, but I held my ground and told her that Hank didn't want to see her anymore, and neither did Ella.

She started crying at this point, trying to trick me, but I didn't fall for it.

I told her that we were having a dinner party and she was cordially *not* invited. "Americans only," I said.

She pointed to my scar and asked me what happened to my head, I guess because Hank hadn't told her, and so I filled her in on what the US government had done to me. She got tired of that story quickly, because she doesn't give two rat shits about the USA, let alone its combat veterans. I know because in the middle of my story, she interrupted, saying she was staying at the Four Seasons, and to please have Hank contact her as soon as possible. Her fickle ass suddenly wanted to be part of my family again.

I asked her if sex with a global warming theorist had cooled down, which I thought was a pretty good joke, but she didn't acknowledge it. She just got in the cab, and it drove away.

I went back inside and tried to enjoy the dinner party, but I kept feeling as though I had done something wrong, even though I knew letting Femke into Hank's home would have absolutely destroyed our melting-pot dinner. My mind was certain that Hank would be better off with Sue, but my heart kept asking questions, especially since I knew Ella had been doing a lot of crying about missing her mother. Her sobbing had woken me up in the middle of the night a few times, and that was awful. It sounded like someone was trying to kill her in her bed, and it reminded me of the many times Jessica's crying woke me up.

Hank always beat me to Ella's room, and he was pretty good at calming her and getting her back to sleep, but I knew it was wearing my son down, being both father and mother, especially since he had to take care of his mentally fucked-up father too, who was always having seizures and ending up in the hospital talking to crooks and skiers.

To be honest, I can't remember anything about the rest of that dinner party. I was too lost in my thoughts, debating whether I had done the right thing, blocking Femke from entering Hank's home and keeping Ella from the hug and kiss she wanted so desperately from her biological Dutch mother. A few times my friends asked me if anything was wrong. I kept blaming it on the meds, until finally I said good night to everyone and went to bed.

The next thing I knew it was three a.m., and I was awake again, feeling like I had done something wrong. I went into Hank's bedroom and poked him. He didn't wake up so I poked him harder. That made him sit up and say, "Ella? Are you okay?"

When he turned on the light and saw it was me, he started to get a little pissed off, which made telling him about Femke even harder. Finally I just spilled the beans, letting him know that Femke was at the Four Seasons, and that she had tried to invade our dinner party, but I had told her she wasn't welcome.

Hank closed his eyes and gritted his teeth for a good minute. Finally I asked if he was okay, and that's when he started to say he couldn't "do this anymore," over and over again, like he was having a breakdown himself. I didn't know what to say, so I just stood there.

When Hank started to cry, I got agitated, especially when he asked if any of my friends would mind looking after me for a few days. I said I could just go home for a while if he needed his space, but Hank said NO in a forceful way that made me jump.

I could tell he was really struggling here, and that he thought I might start World War III if I was left home alone with all of my guns. Just to ease his mind, I told him I could probably spend a few days with my old Vietnam buddy Frank, the multimillionaire I told you about before. Hank said that would be great, so I got on it right away.

In the guest room I called Frank's home number, but I got his wife instead. "Goddamn it, Geneva," she said. "I told you never to call here again!"

Geneva was Frank's younger mistress, who he kept in a fancy skyscraper apartment downtown at Two Liberty Place.

I told Frank's wife, Lynn, that it was David Granger calling, and that I was in the middle of an emergency. Because that bitch Lynn hates me, she hung up immediately.

I hesitated before I called back. When Frank came to visit me in the hospital, he didn't like the way I was treating the stupid nurses and doctors, and we got into a little fight about that. We hadn't spoken since. So I was a little surprised when my phone started buzzing, and it was Frank.

He asked if I was okay, and so I told him all about Femke's surprise return and how the windmilling, wooden-clog-wearing motherfucker had forced me out of my current living arrangement with my son.

"Why don't you just go home?" Frank asked, so I told him that my son thought I was "a danger to myself and others," and even though that was bullshit, Hank was under a lot of stress and I didn't want him to worry about me.

Frank asked me what I wanted from him, and I asked if we could just spend some time together maybe and could we use his mistress's apartment, being that she was probably in the Caribbean doing a photo shoot anyway, because she was a model who spent most of the winter half naked in the tropics.

When he didn't answer, I told him that I wouldn't be calling if I wasn't in a really fucked-up place, and then I told him about how I sort of blanked out during dinner too, and maybe it would be good to be around another veteran for a few days. I had done the same for him many times whenever his bitch wife kicked him out of his mansion on the Main Line. He knew he owed me for that and more, so I just waited for him to man up, which he eventually did.

"Jesus Christ," Frank said, and then he told me to meet him in the Two Liberty Place lobby in an hour.

I could hear Hank crying in his room, talking to Femke on the phone. I didn't want to wake up Ella. I left my son a note on the dinner table saying I'd be with Frank, so there was nothing to worry about, and then I called a cab.

The driver was a white guy, but he smelled pretty bad anyway. Kept farting and stinking up the whole car, which was just my luck. I didn't tip him shit when we arrived at the shiny skyscraper.

I lit up a cigarette on the sidewalk. The cabdriver hung around staring at me, trying to shame me for being cheap, so I walked back over to him and motioned for him to roll down the window. When he did, I said, "No one tips a farting cabdriver, so do yourself a favor and go get yourself some TUMS."

He drove away, and I was left alone with my Marlboro Light.

I don't know if you've ever had the opportunity to smoke a cigarette on a city sidewalk just as the sun is coming up, but it is truly a magnificent experience. Hardly any cars on the streets. No pedestrians. A heavy quiet fills all of the spaces between the buildings, like one of Jessica's blank canvases before she filled it up with all of the demons in her mind. I love smoking a cigarette in predawn Philadelphia. You don't even need a gun to feel safe. One of the few great joys of my life, and so I had five or six smokes, switching hands, so that one could get warm in a pocket while the other allowed me to keep puffing, until Frank's limo rolled up and he popped out in a suit and tie covered by a cashmere overcoat, all of which probably cost more than you make in a year.

"I see you came dressed up," he said. I was in full camouflage, and he knew that meant things weren't good in my mind.

I just nodded, and then we got some takeout coffee and went on up to his mistress's apartment, which is better than any suite in any top hotel in the world. All leather furniture. Persian rugs, which, like I said, are classy. Sophisticated art that Frank buys off Hank, just to support his friend's son.

I should probably say that Frank claims to merely mentor Geneva. He says he has never fucked her and is fond of bringing attention to the fact that he is forty years her senior. But I think everyone—including Frank's wife—knows that you don't buy a one-point-five-million-dollar apartment for a woman you only mentor. No, you buy that sort of apartment for a model who has agreed to bump uglies with you on a regular basis, but that remains none of my business, so I don't really discuss it with Frank.

Even though it was early in the morning and neither of us had eaten, Frank broke out two Cohiba Esplendidos, which meant we were going to have a proper man talk. We did that out on the balcony, where there are heat lamps and these real bearskin blankets made from bears that Frank had actually shot and killed himself.

Once we had the sticks going and the air was full of Cuban smoke, I let loose with some of my theories on the government and its connection to my brain surgery, outlining how the doctors were on the take and how the VA was no fucking help whatsoever, and Frank just sat there puffing away, looking out over Philadelphia from under his bearskin blanket and nodding every now and then. When our cigars were almost kicked, I realized that I had been talking for almost an hour and Frank hadn't said a single word, so I asked him what he thought.

He said I should have gone back to Vietnam with him, because it would have given me closure. I told him I couldn't and never would be able to go.

Then he brought up Clayton Fire Bear, which sort of caught

me by surprise, since I didn't even really remember telling Frank about that no-good red Indian motherfucker. I mentioned him to you a few times already. Fire Bear was the one who used to scalp Vietcong.

"You really still have Fire Bear's knife in your possession?" Frank asked when I didn't say anything. "You kept saying his name in the hospital when you first woke up. You asked me to locate Fire Bear when I visited you postsurgery. Do you remember telling me about the knife?"

I didn't remember telling Frank to locate Fire Bear, nor did I remember anything else about my postoperation experience, but I sure as shit still had that big Indian's knife, and I told Frank so.

"Don't you think you should give it back?" he said. Frank was always harping on closure when it came to me and all things Vietnam, so this conversation didn't surprise me one bit. And yet he really didn't understand the full scope of what he was asking me to do.

Back in Vietnam, you could smell death and decay wherever Clayton Fire Bear went, because of the crusty Vietcong scalps hanging from his belt. I don't even think his kind of Indian used to scalp people back in the day, but Indians sort of got lumped together in the jungle. I don't mean that they stuck all the Indians into separate Indian platoons, but that non-Indian soldiers said the same shit to every Indian they saw in the jungle. We called them all "Chief," which I'd later learn was offensive, and often times Indians would be given more dangerous jobs, like walking point, because everyone thought they had a sixth sense, when they didn't have shit and could die just as easily as your average white soldier who had bought the bullet. And I would later learn that this wore on the Indian soldiers and made them feel low and excluded. So not only were they dealing with all the stress of fighting yellow men in the jungle, they also had to manage the misinformed expectations of their fellow US soldiers who had watched too many Hollywood cowboys and Indians on TV.

I'm not going to tell you what tribe Clayton Fire Bear belongs to, nor am I going to tell you his real name, because he and I now have an understanding that I will not violate.

I really did have the hunting knife Fire Bear used on his Vietcong victims. It's housed in a beautiful leather sheath with his real last name written on it in what looks like fading green Magic Marker. It has a bone handle. Six inches of silver shine like a mirror. Out of habit, I always kept it sharp enough to split a hair. That knife had been with me for almost fifty years, and here is the official story of how it came to be in my possession:

Back in the Vietnam jungle, when everyone finally got sick of the putrid smell of rotting human scalps, my superiors, in all their infinite wisdom, one day put me in charge of disciplining Clayton Fire Bear. From above came these orders: "Break the wild Indian."

On the particular base where this all went down, there was a raised platform of sorts where all of the men used to play cards and smoke. This wasn't top construction, to say the least. The cracks were wide, and cigarette butts would fall through between the wooden boards.

After I confiscated Fire Bear's weapons, I made him strip. Then I tied the big Indian's hands behind his back and, at gunpoint, made him slither around in the sand like a snake, wearing nothing but tighty-whities, picking up with his teeth—one at a time—all of the butts under the platform. Fire Bear had to lift his head high enough to deposit each butt into a metal bucket that the Vietnamese jungle sun had heated up enough to burn lips and cheeks. There were hundreds of sandy tar-filled butts, and the nipple-chafing task took all day. By the time he was done, Fire Bear was caked in sweat and dirt, his lips were crisscrossed with burns, and he couldn't even stand without help.

On his feet again, Fire Bear—gasping for breath and half delirious—asked for his knife back.

I examined the weapon more closely.

Rumor was, it was a genuine bear-bone handle. From the first bear my Indian nemesis had ever killed. His father made the knife for him to signify he had officially stepped over the thin line that separates boys and men, or some such mystical Indian shit.

"What kind of bear?" I asked.

"Fuck you," he said.

I had my orders, and so I kept the knife. Everyone was sick and tired of Fire Bear scalping pajama wearers, myself included. Plus he had disobeyed direct orders from above and needed to be put in his place. I did what I did for his own damn good.

Fire Bear looked directly into my eyes and threatened to kill me if I kept the knife. He said he was going to do it in the future, when I least expected it—maybe even after the war ended, so the soil of his ancestors could drink my blood.

His Indian mumbo-jumbo didn't scare me one bit. Using the bear-bone knife, I cut the rope that bound Fire Bear's hands and offered him a drink of water. He guzzled the entire canteen, spit on the ground, and, after he finally caught his breath, he again promised to kill me.

That big Indian pulled his hair straight up, raised a finger to his forehead, and made the scalping motion. I stared him right back in his dark evil eyes and said, "I'll be waiting for your red ass. Scalp me if you can. But you better make sure you finish the job, because I'll end you if you don't."

When I released him, Clayton Fire Bear immediately went AWOL—vanished into the jungle foliage—and I never did see him in Vietnam again. But that didn't mean the gooks got him. A lot of soldiers disappeared in the jungle from time to time, only to reemerge when we least expected.

Regardless, Fire Bear took up full-time residence in my mind. Sometimes he whispered death threats; other times he'd plead his case. He hadn't done a goddamn thing to me. Without explanation, my superiors told me to break the Indian, and I obeyed, just like I followed orders when they said kill all the yellow men. I didn't ask questions in the jungle. Little did I know I'd be asking questions for the rest of my life.

I next saw Clayton Fire Bear in Kansas, right before they threw me into their secret loony bin. Like I said before, he was at Fort Riley. I saw him off in the distance—I was sure it was him on account of how fucking tall he was, and there weren't a whole lot of Indians around, let alone tall ones. So I knew he had made it back alive to the States.

"I spent decades wishing I had killed Clayton Fire Bear

when I had the chance," I told Frank as we sat on his mistress's balcony, overlooking the City of Brotherly Love. "I used to see him in the shadows everywhere I went."

"Yeah, well, I located him." Frank put the nub of his cigar into the crystal ashtray, which signified that he was finished, because he never puts his cigar down until he is done. "Like you asked me to do. I think the surgery reminded you that we're all running out of time."

"What do you mean?" I asked.

"You need to make peace with Clayton Fire Bear," Frank said, and then added that I still had something that didn't belong to me, a big something, probably sacred to an Indian—the knife his father had made for him. And Clayton Fire Bear's father was most likely dead now, which heightened the significance. Then Frank went on to say Fire Bear was still alive and living out west, but like I said before, I'm not saying where so that I can protect the innocent.

The investigators Frank had hired said that Fire Bear wasn't exactly scalping people anymore. He was a successful lawyer who had started his own firm, now twenty or so attorneys strong. I have to admit that I was proud of Clayton Fire Bear for making something of his life in America, especially considering he was Indian on top of being all fucked up by the Vietnam War.

I don't want to take anything away from the blacks who have survived slavery, but America has most definitely fucked the Indians too. Try to think of a black celebrity who has more money than you do. I bet you can think up a pretty long list. Now name a single Native American who is likely to have more money than you. The list gets a lot smaller, right? Our government tried to *exterminate* the Indians, and while the fucking scumbag Nazi party is no longer in power, the US government keeps rolling strong. I'm not rooting for America to fail anytime soon, don't get me wrong here, but these sorts of thoughts keep this American patriot up at night.

Frank was pushing me pretty hard to give back the knife, but while I was sympathetic to the historic plight of Indians here in the USA, my taking Fire Bear's prize possession had nothing to do with his being an Indian and everything to do with exerting dominance over an out-of-control motherfucker in the jungle. If you don't establish absolute total control over out-of-control motherfuckers when you are at war, you risk being killed or even worse.

Also, being that I am considerate, I was actually concerned for Fire Bear's current mental health. If I just showed up wearing camouflage one day, wanting to return the knife I took off him in the jungle fifty fucking years ago, I was definitely risking setting him off again, triggering all sorts of dark shit.

Frank didn't understand PTSD triggers because he never really did any fighting in Vietnam. He was always building things and doing positive stuff that still makes him feel good to this day.

But there was one thing that had me interested in visiting Fire Bear that was hard to talk about. I tried to shield Jessica from a lot of the specific details I had experienced in Vietnam, because she already had enough horror-show shit playing between her ears, and so I never told her the worst parts, let alone names. I'm pretty sure I didn't tell her that a huge motherfucking Indian had sworn to track me down and scalp me stateside. I wouldn't have wanted Jessica to worry about that. And she absolutely would have, especially toward the end, when she really lost it.

You probably already know exactly what happened to Jessica because it was in all the papers and you surely have access to those, and I also know you sneaky motherfuckers have been spying and keeping a file on me for decades too. This is all surely in there, but just to set the record straight, I don't think Jessica was ever cut out for motherhood.

After Hank was born, her depression worsened, even though I bought her a nice house and had the garage made into a studio for her and then stocked it with all of the best painting supplies money could buy.

When she was pregnant, we made love all the time. But once Hank came, that stopped completely. The doctors had told us that it takes some time to heal, and I was completely okay with that—willing to wait, taking Molly Palm and her five sisters out on private dates, if you know what I mean. But after eight or so months passed and it was clear that Jessica no longer wanted to have sex, I knew there was a big fucking problem.

She did her best to be a good mother. Tried hard not to let Hank see what she was feeling on the inside. Instead she wore a mask daily until I'd come home from work. She had to serve us dinner and then put Hank to bed, but just as soon as our son's bedroom lights were out, the smile would vanish and the crying would begin.

The only thing that seemed to cure the sadness back then,

in the early seventies, was the painting, so I would tell her to paint. I'd even wash and dry the dishes all by myself, even when the game was on TV, just so she could escape into her art.

That worked for a few years, until Hank started to walk and talk and look like his biological father. The boy was so eager to please his mother, you almost got to feeling like he was trying to atone for the evil that brought him into the world. Little Hank would keep his room neater than any child should, always putting away his toys without being told. Bathing and brushing his teeth on schedule. Constantly washing his hands. Never getting his clothes dirty, because he never wanted to roughhouse with the other boys in the neighborhood. Hank was the quintessential momma's boy, within eyesight of Jessica all day and night, wanting to help her. People used to praise Hank for being good, but he was *too* good, and Jessica knew it.

They both loved art, and I used to love watching them sketch and paint together in Hank's room or at the dining room table. But somewhere along the line, Jessica stopped wanting to share her escape with our son. I think it might have been when he started painting his mother obsessively. Hank might have been in the third or fourth grade. He painted more than a hundred or so portraits of her—none of them very good, and all of them depicting Jessica looking tired and sad and defeated. It was like the boy somehow knew what was coming, and it frightened my wife. She'd ask Hank why she never looked happy in his paintings, and he'd say he painted what he saw, just like she taught him to do. After a few months of this, Jessica forbid him to paint any more portraits of her, ripping the most recent one down from the refrigerator. Hank burst into tears, and Jessica locked herself in her studio for two days. I don't even think she ate. When she finally emerged and rejoined our household, she was distant.

I'm not going to go on and on about how fucking brilliant my wife was, nor will I describe all of her many wonderful paintings, and I mean that literally—they were full of wonder, even the frightening ones—because going into detail about her portfolio would take up ten thousand pages of this report. I'll just tell you about the best one she did very early on, which she titled *The Reason You're Alive*. It might have been the first painting she made in that studio of hers.

You might think I'm vain when I tell you about my favorite of Jessica's, because it's a portrait of me. Baby Hank's in there too. I'm in my full Vietnam combat gear, decked out in camouflage with a rifle strapped to my back, and I'm in the jungle with all sorts of bad shit around me—gooks in trees, tigers, unidentifiable snakes, because Jessica didn't know all that much about the specific snakes they had in Vietnam, napalm fire, and part of the jungle is even melting from Agent Orange.

But in the middle of everything, I'm not fighting; I'm holding little naked Hank, whose umbilical cord is still connected to his stomach. If you follow the cord with your eyes, you will see that it turns into a bubble that surrounds Hank and me and seems to be shielding us from all of that bad shit in Vietnam.

It was heavily influenced by Henri Rousseau, to say the least. And you don't have to go to art appreciation school to understand the symbolism in that or any of Jessica's paintings, which is why my wife is so much better than artists like Eggplant X and other bozos who just want to make money and be mysterious asshole celebrities trying to make people guess what the fuck their paintings mean and then making everyone feel stupid when they get it wrong. Jessica never wanted to show her paintings to anyone, let alone sell them. I'm pretty sure they would have commanded millions on the open market. But she just wanted to paint. Period. *Needed* to paint. It kept her alive for ten years of motherhood. She never really wanted to be a mother.

When she let me see *The Reason You're Alive*, I didn't cry but I got a big old lump in my throat. She had captured me perfectly—not just the way I looked, either, but how I felt damned, and yet I was still trying my hardest to atone. I was allowed to see the painting three or four more times before it went into Jessica's archives, which meant that it was stacked up with all the other paintings, and no one was allowed to touch any of them. I had always dreamed that Jessica would one day get up the courage to show her art, maybe after Hank grew up and she was older and had matured as an artist or when she had finally beaten her depression, but that never happened.

A few years later, things got really bad, only I didn't catch it in time.

I knew Jessica was having more difficulty pretending that she wanted to be a mother to Hank, but I was climbing up the corporate ladder at the bank I was working at in the city, which often meant after-work drinks and golf outings and dinners at expensive restaurants that Jessica never wanted to go to. And her reclusiveness was doing zilch for my career. The wife of a banker is supposed to schmooze, and all the other wives at the bank were fucking pros. So I was handicapped.

I thought the art supplies and garage were enough, but one night in December of 1980 I took Hank to a 76ers game, and when we came home there were fire trucks and police cars everywhere. Our house was fine, but Jessica's studio had burned to the ground, which meant all of her paintings had been destroyed. My heart sank. I knew this would send her over the edge, into an even deeper depression. But then I saw the haunted looks that the cops and firefighters were giving me.

There are no words to describe how I felt, losing Jessica, so I'm not even going to try here.

She seemed so happy when we left her that night. I've since heard that's a classic sign for depressed people who are about to commit suicide: it means their suffering is about to end. Jessica kissed us both in the kitchen before we exited the house through the back door in the kitchen. Her last words to us were "Have a great time at the game!"

Just as soon as he understood what had happened, standing there with all the fire trucks and hoses and sad-looking cops, Hank started to apologize. He kept saying he was sorry, like he had lit the fire, which he obviously hadn't. At the time I was trying to process everything—the horrific fact that my wife burned herself to death, using her own art as a funeral pyre. But later I'd hear Hank apologizing for his mother's death in my mind. I still hear it sometimes. It's a whisper that's ever-present, like my own heartbeat. *I'm sorry. I'm sorry. I'm sorry.*

I probably should have talked more with Hank about his mother's suicide. Today a kid like that would get therapy. But it was a long time ago, and you people trained me to keep my mouth shut and soldier on, which is exactly what I did, right or wrong. Young Hank followed my lead there, and time kept passing.

Burning yourself alive is a hell of a way to go. I have spent all my time since blaming myself for what had happened, even though the VA shrink I currently see and four or five other headshrinkers have all told me it's not my fault so many times over the decades that followed.

But I know this is God paying me back for killing so many gook civilians and burning so many villages. No matter how much I might not like it, God likes humans, even Communist gooks, better than dogs, and that is the exact reason why God put the bad thoughts in Jessica's brain. After all I had done during the war, I would never be allowed happiness, no matter how many good deeds I did for the rest of my life. Everyone who didn't understand God's math said I should remarry, but I never could go through all that again. Wouldn't want to bring another woman down. And Jessica was the only one for me, anyway.

The reason I went into all of this stuff here is that a few weeks after Jessica burned herself to death, I was emptying out her bureau, getting rid of her clothes, when I saw Clayton Fire Bear's real name carved into the bottom of her underwear drawer. The letters were big white blocks, like he had cut to the bone of the stained wood. Since she had never even heard it, Jessica couldn't have carved that name into the drawer bottom, although she would have surely seen it every time she put her laundry away. It was a mystery that I wasn't sure I wanted to solve at first, especially since the firefighters had confirmed without a doubt, using their firefighter science, that my wife had intentionally started the blaze and made no attempt to escape it, but rather *chose* to go up in smoke with her art. Try living with that on your fucking conscience.

I've asked all the VA shrinks—and I've seen more than a few over the years—why Jessica didn't just leave Hank and me and start a new life if she hated ours so much. They all say leaving doesn't kill what's inside. And I know that's true because I left the Vietnam jungle so many years ago.

And I damn near went insane trying to figure out how Fire Bear's name came to be carved into my wife's underwear drawer, which is creepy enough, but downright disturbing when you factor in all of the other shit I have already told you about.

But on the balcony, as I took the last few puffs of the Cohiba, Frank was telling me this monster Indian from my past was now a well-respected lawyer who would probably very much appreciate having his father's knife back. And the truth I wasn't telling Frank was that I wouldn't mind knowing if Fire Bear had been in my house. And when. How. Why.

Regardless, we could agree on one thing: I needed closure.

13.

After everything that happened, first my fucked-up brain and then Hank kicking me in the balls by falling back in love with that traitorous Dutch export of a woman—and after all the father-son progress we had made in Femke's absence!—I didn't feel much like hunting down a gigantic Indian lawyer who may or may not still have wanted to scalp me.

I wasn't afraid of Clayton Fire Bear. Never was. Never will be. But facing that past was fucking daunting, which is a common thing for most veterans, not just Vietnam vets.

And so instead, Frank and I had a few days of living like bachelor kings, during which we smoked Cubans in this underground cigar room in the city that Frank knows the secret password for and ate steaks at the Union League, which tried to not let me in, on account of the fact that I was wearing camouflage and not a proper suit and tie. But Frank has so much money that he can basically do whatever he wants anywhere, and so—especially since I was a US veteran—they finally made an exception and even let me keep my camouflage bucket hat on while I devoured my filet mignon. We went to the shooting range and squeezed off a bunch of rounds, which is great for dealing with stress. They always hang up pictures of Muslim terrorists as targets, so it feels patriotic to kill those paper bastards too. We even took the limousine to Atlantic City, because Frank likes to play craps. He bets so much money, we always draw a crowd, and the hottest babes around fight to blow on Frank's dice. The more money you have, the hotter the women you attract. Period. At night we'd watch the games until I'd pass out, and then Frank did who knows what.

I was having a really good time with my best white non-homo friend, but after a few days, I think we both sort of got sick of each other. He asked if there was anyone else who could take a turn making sure I wasn't a danger to myself or others, and that's when I called Sue.

When she answered, she said that I was just the person she needed to speak with because she had a favor to ask of me. Then she warned it was a big favor—the kind that had to be asked in person.

I figured I'd say yes to her favor before I asked her if she could watch me for a few days, and we agreed to meet at a coffee shop not too far from the Liberty skyscrapers.

When I walked into the coffee shop, I was blinded by the huge diamond on Sue's left ring finger, and that confused me. I started to get my hopes up for Hank. Maybe he really did have the balls to stand up to Femke and woo Sue. As I strode over to the table, I began to imagine having a true American patriot for a daughter-in-law, and my heart filled up with pride to the point of bursting.

Sue was beaming, and she couldn't even stay seated. She popped up out of the booth, threw both hands around my neck, and kissed my cheek, which surprised me because she had never done anything like that before. I got a whiff of her, and there was that vanilla and lavender.

Sue held up her ring finger and said, "Surprise!"

The gigantic rock must have cost at least twenty grand. My immediate thought was this: I hope my dumbass son had insured it.

I told Sue I couldn't be happier for her as we sat down.

She started acting like she had snorted a mountain of cocaine. She couldn't sit still for a second and was waving her little arms all over the place. Finally she reached across the table and grabbed my hands, and then she said she wanted me to give her away at the altar, because her father was no longer with us, and Alan would have wanted a fellow Vietnam veteran to do the job.

It took a lot of strength to keep the tears from escaping my eyes. I realized that I had not yet agreed to give her away on her big day when she said, "*Will you?*"

I nodded once, and a great big tear fell from my cheek and splattered on the table, so I looked at my lap and tried to regain my composure.

Then Sue said that there was one more part to all of this. Teddy had traditional values, and since Sue thought of me as a father figure, he wanted to take me out to dinner, tell me all about his ten-year plan, and outline exactly how he would provide a good life for Sue and their future children.

This is when I looked up and said, "Did you say *Teddy*?"

And she confirmed that she *had* said Teddy. She said she told me about this Teddy a million times before my brain surgery, only when I was waking up post-op, I had told her not to mention Teddy to me ever again, because he wasn't good enough for her.

I don't remember saying that, nor did I even remember Sue being in the room with me during my recovery. I only remember her coming a few days after the surgery, but she said she was with me at the hospital the whole time. We'll have to chalk the blanks in my memory up to your evil employer cutting out part of my brain and the people-cutter skier's abominable incompetence.

I kept asking questions, because it seemed like Sue was trying to trick me, but I could tell from the look on her face that she was deeply in love with this Teddy, whoever the fuck he was.

So I went ahead and asked her directly if she had any feelings whatsoever for Hank, and she said she thought of me as a father, so Hank was like a brother to her. She wanted to get to know Hank and Ella better, and she knew that Teddy and Hank would be good friends too, so I had to think of it as positive growth in the family.

"How come you've never introduced me to Teddy?" I said.

There were two reasons.

First, she knew I wanted her to fall in love with Hank, so she was afraid of disappointing me, especially while I was recovering. Apparently Sue and Hank had even talked about this when I fell asleep after the dinner parties. Hank was actually the one who talked her into introducing Teddy to me, which makes him a true moron, not fighting for the better of the two women available to him.

The second reason she didn't introduce me to Teddy was because I already knew him, and he was sort of nervous about asking someone he respected so much for Sue's hand in marriage. Apparently, he had finally gotten up the courage to approach me right around the time I had that first seizure and totaled the BMW. But he didn't want to bother me in the hospital or while I was recovering, especially since I was in such bad shape at first.

I kept racking my damaged brain, trying to think of someone I knew named Teddy, but I couldn't come up with a single face. I thought maybe I was losing even more of my memory, so I stayed quiet.

Finally, Sue said that Teddy was waiting outside and was going to join us for coffee right then. That made my heart beat faster, because I didn't want to see someone I had forgotten. That would have been fucking awkward, especially since this man was going to marry my unofficial daughter.

But then "Teddy" walked into the coffee shop with that swagger of his, and I knew exactly who he was.

Big T.

I didn't know him as Teddy, because none of his gym homeboys called him that, and he went by Theodore in the banking world.

Teddy doesn't really sound like a black dude's name until you remember Teddy Pendergrass, who was one smooth brother. "Turn Off the Lights" is a track that can get you laid instantly with the right sort of woman.

On the basketball court Sue's Teddy was known as Big T, so I used that moniker as I stood up and did the secret brother handshake with him. At the end of this particular handshake you pull each other closer with your fists locked together between your chests, which keeps you at least four inches apart so it doesn't become a homo handshake, and then you pound your other fist on your brother's back three times before you let go. I performed it flawlessly. Big T gave me a huge grin.

We all sat down, and Big T told me he loved Sue with all his heart even before he found out that she had an American hero for a father figure, and so I told him that Alan was the true hero, bringing Sue to America and raising her the right way, which was what you should always look for when shopping for a wife, and that bit made Sue a little mad, which is when I remembered that it wasn't just me and Big T, but a woman was also present.

Then Big T made a big deal about my putting a good word in for him at PNC Bank, where he currently works as an executive, making big-time coin, which is another reason why I approve of him for Sue. Big T was a true moneymaker, and he was also appreciative and, even better, loyal. He kept saying the phone call I had made changed his life, and I kept telling him it was living his life the right way—working hard and locking down many smart, opportunistic plays—that made making the phone call a pleasure. Long-term success usually comes from consistently hitting singles and doubles, not from hitting the occasional home run every so many games. Big T got that and therefore was a real man by anyone's standards—always willing to do the little necessary things to help the team win rather than swinging selfishly for the fences.

"Why exactly *did* you make that call?" asked Sue.

I told her all of the above and then added this: Big T was also the first brother at the health club who ever let me run ball. He vouched for me with his people, so I returned the favor.

Big T—who was dressed in an expensive suit, by the way, looking pro and classy—went on to say that when he found out about my relationship with Sue, he was worried that I wouldn't approve.

I told him I wasn't a fucking racist, which made both him and Sue laugh.

"No, G.I. Joe," he said, using his brother rhymes. "I thought maybe you'd think I put my hand in your cookie jar too many times. And so I wanted to prove myself worthy first."

This is when he told me about the huge promotion he had received at PNC Bank, letting me know that he was now one of the highest-ranking bankers in the building, thanking me for the help. I told him that my phone call was just a door opener. "They don't promote idiots," I said. "You did all the work yourself."

I had a thought right then that mixed-race babies are often the cutest babies, and a lot of beautiful people are mixed race. And so I knew that Sue and Big T were going to make gorgeous children, all of whom I hoped would call me Pop Pop. And I had a hard time holding the tears back for a second time.

Sue spent the night at my home, making sure I wasn't a danger to myself or others and admiring my large gun collection, and then I went out with Big T the next night.

He took me to the Capital Grille for steak, because he knows how to eat right, and he went over his finances and his ten-year plan with me. He had a pretty good portfolio for a man his age and had managed to even buy some properties at the right time in neighborhoods that were up-and-coming, so I told him about Gay Johnny, for two reasons.

One, if Teddy was going to be my unofficial son-in-law, I wanted only the top players in Philly to be handling his business.

Two, I knew that the brothers were sometimes too hard on the gays, and I wanted to make sure he was not against them.

Big T didn't blink. Instead he said, "I'm down for a meet-and-greet," rhyming again, and proving to me that he wouldn't have a problem with Johnny and Timmy.

As we were eating huge pieces of chocolate cake with vanilla ice cream, he said that he was going to take me to his "crib" because it was his turn to "keep me out of trouble," as he put it, and if it was okay, he wanted to introduce me to his family in the morning.

That was fine with me.

When the bill came, we both reached for it, but the little black waitress's hand was headed toward Big T, so I said, "I'll take that. This is my new son."

Big T smiled at the waitress, and she smiled back in a bitchy sort of way. Then she asked me how one gets a *new* son, so I told her that Big T was marrying my daughter.

The waitress gave Big T a really dirty look as she handed me the bill, and so I asked him why.

He explained that she probably thought my daughter was white, and that black women don't like it when "their men marry blond-haired blue-eyed Barbie."

So I reminded him that my daughter was yellow, with eyes that were so brown they looked black, and he said a lot of black women don't like that either, because they want their men, especially their successful men, to stay black.

I could see the logic in that from the point of view of the black women. And so I asked Big T to explain all of this to my dumb liberal son when they met, because Hank didn't have the first clue when it came to how racism really worked, and had stupidly ended up marrying into one of the worst races imaginable: the Dutch.

Big T laughed and then asked, "What do you have against the Dutch?"

His challenge forced me to admit that I had only really ever gotten to know three Dutch people, none of whom I liked.

And that's when Big T said I was racist against my own people, but joking around in a philosophical sort of way.

I told him I wasn't Dutch.

So he asked me, what country in Africa did I think his ancestors were from? I couldn't tell him. "So we're all African, but you're not European?" It was a fair point, and I told him so. This new son of mine is no dummy.

Big T drove Mercedes-Benz, and on the way to his crib, I thought about how much more I liked eating dinner with him than with my actual son, which made me feel ashamed. Big T liked sports and good food and could debate race relations without sounding like an ignoramus, and even though Hank would fully "admit his privilege," I don't think you could find three American men of any racial background who would pick Hank over Big T in a who-is-a-real-man contest.

"You all right, old man whitey?" Big T asked as he drove.

"I'm straight," I said, using brother language.

And then we were at his crib, which was off South Street in a small building he owned. There were six or seven little apartments, all occupied by people paying rent to Big T. My new black son was running work, and I was prouder and prouder with every new bit of info he revealed about himself.

Inside, all of his furniture was leather. Nice-looking, sleek, modern. He had a huge TV, and he flipped on some basketball right away, but I was too tired to hang and told him so, explaining that it was all the fucking meds.

He laughed and said I was to sleep in his bed, but I protested.

"What? You're too proud to sleep in a black man's sheets?" Big T said with this angry expression on his face that I had never seen before.

I didn't know what to say, and had one of those awkward white-people moments that didn't exist even ten years ago.

But then he said he was just playing with me and then added that he *insisted* I sleep in his bed. He had washed the aforementioned sheets, and he was just fine on the couch.

He said, "If you have another seizure you could fall off the couch and crack your head open on the coffee table," which was thoughtful and probably true.

And so we did the handshake again, after which I said good night and went into his bedroom.

He had a nice king-size bed that was very normal looking. No leopard-skin blankets or black fists on the walls or red-green-and-black Africa cutouts or anything like that. It could have been any successful white person's room anywhere in America, which was sort of a disappointment in some ways, because you would think a brother would have more style than that.

As I lay in Big T's bed, I began to see that Sue and Big T were making a real commitment to me, involving me in their wedding plans and looking out for me as my fucked-up brain healed. If you toss in my favorite queer couple, you might start to think I had all the family I needed for the rest of my life, even without Hank. I could swallow that pill if it weren't for Ella, and so I realized that I had to make things right with Hank somehow.

Frank's words echoed in my head, and that was fucking me up, because I didn't want to deal with that Indian motherfucker Clayton Fire Bear. And yet I could see that closure was necessary. I was slipping, and my mind was no longer even sound enough to be left alone with firearms. I also needed to give the knife back. Deep down I knew that was a mission I still needed to accomplish. I'm not sure why, but right then and there, in Big T's bed, I decided I'd do it.

I slept better than I had in decades.

I woke up at five a.m. like always and found Big T stretching in the kitchen. He told me he was going out for a jog, and I nodded and smiled. That's a real man right there. Up by five. Seizing the day.

He asked if I was cool, and I said, "Always," so we went outside and I watched him jog down the street as I sparked up my first cigarette of the day on the sidewalk and the sun rose over the City of Brotherly Love.

Everything seemed okay in that good early-morning moment, like it always does.

And then I remembered my promise.

"Fire Bear," I said.

14.

Sue showed up at Big T's apartment, and we all got in the Mercedes and drove down to Delaware. His parents lived in a pretty nice house in a little suburban neighborhood. The first floor was packed full of their family and friends. Sue and I were the only nonblacks.

With Big T's dad, I tried to do the only brother handshake I knew, but was surprised to find out the old man didn't know it. When I went in for the part when you bang your fist on the other brother's back, Mr. Baker asked me what the hell I was doing.

Big T made it okay by saying, "This guy's blacker than you, Pop."

Sue was a big hit with the women, who pulled her away from us right away. Just like in white families, all the men gathered around the television to watch sports while the women talked loudly about nothing at all.

I was surprised when one of Big T's uncles put on golf and the room fell silent with each shot. I had seen the occasional brother on the golf course in my day, and I guess Tiger Woods changed everything, but Tiger was only part black, and regardless of all that, I had never been in a living room packed with golf-watching blacks, so a new experience to say the least. His uncles and cousins were wearing argyle sweater vests and prep-school shoes, and it became obvious that Big T was the blackest sheep of the family, so to speak.

The day passed, and there were good eats, as you might expect—the best ribs I had in years. And I ate four pieces of cornbread, because white people are shit at making cornbread, so a honky has to capitalize on such opportunities whenever they come along.

At one point I went looking for the toilet, and upstairs I ran into Big T's father in the hallway. Turns out his name was David too, only he went by Dave.

I asked him if he named his son after Teddy Pendergrass, maybe because he had been listening to some Teddy P when Big T had been conceived.

Dave told me that his son was named after Theodore Roosevelt, and when I asked why, he said he was a history buff and had always liked the name Theodore.

I told him my father had named me after King David in the Bible, and Dave said he wasn't religious.

So I told Dave that I had called in a favor for his son at PNC Bank, and he nodded and said he knew. It was then that I realized Dave might be a little jealous of the good relationship I had with his son.

I asked him where the can was.

"Why are you wearing nothing but camouflage?" he responded.

I told him I had spent some time in the jungle over in Vietnam, and the government had recently cut out part of my brain. I took off my bucket hat and showed him my scar.

He glanced at it and then pointed to the end of the hall, so I hit the head and left it at that.

Then I fell asleep on the couch, watching golf.

On the ride home, Sue and Big T thanked me over and over again for being part of everything. And I got the sense that maybe they felt just as exhausted as I did. I'd caught them looking weary while we were still at the party, and at one point in the afternoon I had seen Big T whispering with his mother and heard Sue's name come up a few times and maybe even heard something about her not being black, which was when I realized that maybe everyone's family had hypocrites and liberals and assholes in it regardless of skin color.

I have to admit that I did not like Big T's parents very much, even if they did put out good ribs and fantastic cornbread. And I could understand why Big T had moved to the city and why he wanted me to be his new father-in-law, who would not discriminate against his wife.

I noticed that Sue and Big T were driving me through Jersey, so I asked why we had come this way.

Sue said they were taking me home to my own house.

I asked if I was healthy enough to spend the night alone, and they assured me that I wouldn't be alone.

I asked who was going to babysit me, and they said they weren't sure, which seemed strange, so I pushed for more answers. Turns out that they had been in contact with Hank, who was calling the shots from afar while he put his life back together with Femke.

I wasn't surprised to see Frank's limousine in my driveway when we pulled in. I said good-bye to Big T and Sue, and as they pulled away, Frank said, "I did it for your own good."

I got a bad feeling. I rushed toward my front door, which was unlocked. I knew exactly what had happened right then and there. I went to my weapons room and found it empty. When I turned around, Frank was standing in the doorway behind me.

He said that he did this, not Hank, which I realized was bullshit right away, primarily because Frank didn't have a key to my house, although he could have easily paid a locksmith to let him in.

"What the fuck?" I said.

Frank said it wasn't as bad as I thought. He hadn't gotten rid of my guns, he had stored them at a private gun range he belonged to, and he and I could go any time we wanted. The only catch was that he had to go with me, and I couldn't take any guns out of the range.

I asked how I knew that my guns wouldn't be stolen. "Come on," he said, meaning he was a billionaire, so any gun range he belonged to would be devoid of thieves and heavily insured.

We got into his limo and we drove past the city and into Pennsylvania, and finally we arrived at a compound of sorts in the woods.

Once I saw the inside of this place—Persian rugs everywhere—I realized it was only for billionaires like Frank who didn't need to steal shit. Frank had bought me a private room and a gun case. All of my weapons were cleaned and oiled and displayed, including the Glock Sue had been holding for me.

Frank told me that my arsenal would be kept there from now on, and that whenever I wanted to shoot, he'd take me—and if a war should break out in America because of the fucking jihadists, he would pick me up fully armed by helicopter, and we'd put our military training to good use.

You should see Frank's helicopter. State-of-the-art, to say the least.

All of this was a really nice gesture that probably cost him an obscene amount of money—but it meant everyone, including my best Vietnam veteran buddy, no longer thought I would be able to have firearms unsupervised ever again, let alone carry.

For a second I caught myself worrying if this would be the end of me, but then I caught a whiff of that motherfucker Death, and that was all I needed to keep myself from buying the bullet. Frank and I put on our hearing protector earmuffs and shot a few hundred dollars' worth of bullets, filling pictures of raghead terrorists with holes, which made everything feel okay.

On the drive back to New Jersey, I asked Frank if he would spend the night at my place, even though I had no more weapons with which to hurt myself or others, and therefore no longer needed a babysitter. "I hate to admit this, but I'm feeling sort of fucked up about a lot of things," I told Frank.

He smiled and said he had taken the liberty of putting a handmade Cuban humidor in my office, stocked full with Cohiba Esplendidos. "They're not all for you, though," he said. "I'm going to smoke my share. Starting tonight."

I nodded my thanks and then turned my head to look out the window, because I felt like I was going to start crying girly-man tears again. I was happy my friend was looking out for me, but I was terrified by the thought of facing my past. And so when Frank and I were smoking cigars, I began to worry I would chicken out on the whole fucking deal. Killing is a lot easier than saying sorry and meaning it, which I was still working up to accomplishing.

15.

The next morning Hank and Ella showed up at my place around eight, which is when I noticed that Frank's limo and driver had also returned.

Frank emerged from the guest room in a suit and tie and reeking of some Italian cologne his mistress had given him. It smelled like a goat had eaten a bowl of potpourri and then pissed into a spray bottle, but I was polite enough not to mention that because I knew his side woman was into this goat-piss stuff.

Instead, I asked him if Geneva was back in town. He smiled and told me he had some "mentoring" to do. I knew this meant he wanted to get his dick wet, and since I hated his wife anyway, I had no problem with Frank getting laid. Especially after all he had done for me recently.

We shook hands the white person way, and he told me not to smoke all of the Cubans without him. Then he and Hank talked outside as Ella burst through my front door and into my arms.

"My mommy is home for good!" she screamed into my ear. It was hard to be bitter about that, when I could plainly see how much joy it gave my granddaughter.

Blood, as they say, is thicker than water. And as you now know, I had no blood left in the world at all. Hank and Ella didn't know that we weren't blood at that point, but regardless, biology always knows the truth. You can't trick it into favoring nonblood—I had learned that long ago with Hank. Femke had me beat in every way there, now that she and Hank had combined their blood and made Ella.

Midmorning, Hank and I took Ella to an ice-skating rink. She loves to skate, and she's actually pretty good, meaning she can go round and round the rink without falling at all, provided that no other asshole kids knock her down, which sometimes happens. Usually Hank would have been out there on the ice with her, only he never wore actual skates; he just sort of shuffled along in his designer shoes that look like sneakers and cost thousands of fucking dollars just because they have European brand names you've never heard of stamped on the sides.

But on this day, Hank stayed with me on the outside of the rink, watching Ella go round and round with all the other kids and dumb goofy parents. I thought Hank was sticking with me because I was still fucked in the head on account of my brain surgery and was still wearing the safety camouflage too, but it turned out that he wanted to have a man-to-man talk.

He started in by saying he felt we had made real progress over the past couple of weeks and that he had enjoyed having me stay at his house, especially because he got to meet my eclectic group of friends.

I sat there listening to all of the compliments, knowing that there would be bad shit on the other side of the forthcoming "but." Finally that "but" was verbalized, which took us to the news that Femke was back in the picture permanently. She had supposedly gotten all of the weatherman-fucking out of her system and was now allegedly ready to become a faithful wife again, and a loving mother too.

Despite everything that had happened, she still somehow had her job at that "sister school," which apparently did not value attendance when it came to its professors skipping entire weeks of class just to satisfy their sexual urges.

I could understand Femke wanting to come back to the greatest country in the world. You'd have to be a fucking moron to pick the Netherlands over America—that was a no-brainer. But I couldn't really understand what was driving her back to Hank. My dumb and financially irresponsible son had not made Femke sign a prenuptial agreement, or at least he got fucking red-faced mad at me when I suggested it, back in the day, so that Dutch bitch could have easily run off with Ella and half of Hank's hard-earned art-selling fortune, despite the fact that she had been unfaithful. My son lacks the killer instinct necessary to turn the tables and fight for a favorable outcome. He's never lawyered up in his entire life.

Right there on the side of the ice-skating rink, Hank told me that he loved Femke enough to forgive her, and that he was doing this for Ella too, because she needed a mother.

I didn't say anything in response. I know when I am beat.

Hank kept talking, trying to convince himself that he was right, saying things about my Jessica and how I would have surely taken her back had she had a "single moment of weakness."

And that's when I put a finger in Hank's face and said his mother's whole goddamn life was one big moment of weakness on account of her depression, but she managed to refrain from fucking other men while we were married.

And that's when Hank said, "But Mom still left us, and she *never* came back. Never. At least Femke returned home."

That sad bit of logic caught me off guard. On one hand, Hank was right. His mother had left us, and I'd never really held her accountable for that, because I loved her so goddamn much.

On the other hand, Jessica's suicide had fucked up my son to the point where he was still unable to see clearly when it came to women, even three decades after his mother's fiery exit from the planet. And I had to blame Jessica a little bit for that, even though I didn't want to.

So I pressed my lips together tightly, trying to keep the fighting words from coming out of my mouth.

I watched Ella push her little feet right and left as she glided around the rink on two shiny blades of steel, mouthing the lyrics to some bubblegum pop song that was playing and I didn't know.

Maybe it would be better for her if her mother never left again. Maybe she would avoid Hank's fate. I didn't know much about how modern families worked. I only knew that I had fucked up my own beyond repair long ago.

"Femke calls me 'Aap,' " I finally said. "She hates me. So I guess I'm out."

Hank went on to say that he had shared with Femke all that he had learned about me, meaning that I exercised and did business with the gays and had a genetically Vietnamese daughter now and was soon to have a black son-in-law too. He said that Femke was impressed with all of the above, because she's a moron who keeps track of these things. I didn't believe that I would ever be able to forgive her, nor would I ever get used to being called Aap, but there was such hope in my son's expression—hope that I hadn't seen for a long time.

And Ella was trying to skate backward and doing a pretty good job of it, even if her legs were shaking because she was nervous. I was proud to see that my granddaughter was at least brave, and that's when I decided that maybe I needed to be a little braver too.

And so I told Hank that I had to go face my nemesis from the Vietnam War so that I could have closure once and for all.

"Clayton Fire Bear?" Hank asked. "The name you kept repeating at the hospital? He was your *nemesis*?"

I nodded and told him about that big Indian motherfucker, only I didn't go into great detail—I told Hank I had stolen an Indian soldier's knife, and I had to return it before the Indian or I died, because it was the right thing to do.

"Should we be saying 'Indian' or 'Native American'?" Hank asked, as if a tomahawk-wielding red man in a full feather headdress might skate by any moment just to answer him.

It was no use trying to explain. Hank had been lucky enough to avoid combat duty, and therefore he wouldn't understand what I have been talking about in this here politically *incorrect* report. He asked a few more dumb civilian questions before I shut him down completely by saying, "Frank understands. He's helping me. It doesn't concern you."

Hank got this wounded look on his face, but there was nothing I could do about that.

We just watched Ella go round and round for another hour or so, and there was part of me that wished we could just stand there watching her for the rest of our lives, free and clear of Femke forever. Your employer taking out a part of my brain had mellowed me a bit, no doubt, although I know that was not the US government's primary intention.

The rest of the day went by in a blur. While Hank and Ella and I were walking through the mall and eating at the food court and then driving home, my thoughts were back in Vietnam, remembering the day when I was ordered to "break the wild Indian."

I kept playing the whole scene over and over again in my head, thinking about what children we both were, and wondering if Fire Bear had actually carved his name in the bottom of Jessica's underwear drawer, and what would happen when I showed up all these years later with his bear-bone knife and all of these questions.

Frank was convinced that it would be good for both of us, but I wasn't so sure. What if Fire Bear still wanted to scalp me?

Hank kept asking me if I was okay, and I kept blaming my distance on the fucking brain meds they had me on, which are exceptionally awful, so that lie was partially true.

Back at my house, while Ella was watching some unicorn princess bullshit on the television and Hank was making an inedible heart-healthy meal, I caught a smoke in the backyard and called Frank.

When he picked up, he was out of breath, which meant he

was either having a heart attack or he had just finished fucking Geneva, since Frank hasn't exercised since high school. That was his business, so I left it alone.

Instead, I called him a motherfucker for getting into my head and fucking with my thoughts, and then I told him I would give the knife back—that I was ready to right that wrong. A lot of bad shit had happened to me recently, and so maybe this would change my luck. Who knew?

Frank said it was absolutely the right thing to do and that he would accompany me. We would even take this private jet he partially owned, so don't give me too much credit for the hardship. "This is going to heal you better than anything the doctors could ever do for you," he said. That wasn't saying much, considering how fucking stupid my neurologists had already proven themselves.

I told Frank that I wanted to do this good deed as soon as possible, and he said we could leave the next day, which is one of the perks of befriending men with obscene amounts of money. A limo would pick me up first thing in the morning.

Hank served me three different kinds of salad for dinner, and nothing else at all—I shit you not. And during salad number two, which was made out of pickled fucking seaweed, I told him I was going away with Frank for a few days, so he wouldn't have to worry about me. Femke would probably be thrilled.

He ignored my comment about Femke and instead wanted to know where exactly I was going, but there was no way to explain it, especially in front of Ella.

"Personal business," I said, "long overdue," and left it at that.

By then I had realized that Hank was talking regularly to all my friends, so I was sure Frank had told my son more than I had. Part of me was grateful for that, because it saved me from doing the hard explaining. But I knew that Frank would give my son the civilian version he could swallow without getting too sick, which is the version we veterans always give civilians, because nine out of ten veterans are truly goddamn compassionate people. We save all the mental suffering for ourselves. Another reason I'm doing this here report too, because I've got to thinking that maybe our protecting you from the truths we soldiers have lived for decades hasn't really done us—or you, for that matter—many favors.

After dinner Hank let Ella watch more television, which was unusual, because he closely monitored her TV consumption. I understood what was going on when Hank motioned toward the back door and then held two fingers up to his lips, meaning, *Let's have a smoke together.* I didn't approve of Hank's new secret smoking habit, like I said before, but I went outside with him anyway, because I needed one myself.

I gave him a Marlboro Light, put another between my lips, and then sparked up both with a plastic throwaway lighter. Just to put Hank's dumb ass in its place, I lifted up my cigarette and said, "Heart healthy."

"One's not going to kill me," Hank said. "And you're not going to buy the bullet anyway, right?"

I was shocked that Hank had used some of my military slang without irony. He had spent his whole life up to that point mocking my service as he tried his hardest to be the opposite of a real man.

He went on to say that he had been too hard on me in the past. Turns out Frank, Timmy and Johnny, Sue, and even Big T had been in my son's ear ever since my surgery, letting him know that he was paying too much attention to my words and not enough attention to my actions.

He said that even Femke was willing to make an effort to heal old wounds and cease calling me Aap if I stopped referring to her as a "tulip cunt" or a "Euro bitch" and stopped pointing out her country's many flaws. That was a tall order for me, but a good place to start when it came to negotiating with the Dutch.

"I don't want to fight anymore, Dad," Hank said. "I just want my family to . . ." And this is when he started crying again, only this time he really lost it, sobbing, covering his eyes, and saying he was sorry, which reminded me of the night Jessica died.

There was part of me that really wanted to put my arm around Hank and tell him that everything would be okay, but neither of my arms would move, and my lips stayed shut too. A lot had happened, and I needed to stay tough if I was going to keep Death at bay.

My brain was still healing. I wasn't strong enough for hugs and froufrou talk at that moment, no matter how much I may have wanted to give my son what he so desperately wanted from me. That's just the way it was. So I puffed on my cigarette and waited for him to finish the boohooing.

He finally did and asked for another cigarette, so I gave him one and put another Marlboro Light between my lips too. I held the flame up to Hank's smoke. The fire illuminated his tear-streaked cheeks, which made me feel ashamed for my son, so I looked away and lit up my own.

We smoked those down in silence, and then Hank popped in some gum and went inside to wash his hands.

I stood out there gathering my thoughts and watching my breath stain the winter air. It was quiet. I could hear the highway traffic in the distance, like wind over the ocean.

Inside I found Ella asleep on the couch and Hank whispering on the phone with Femke, so I went up to bed and thought about all that had happened. I truly could have thought all night, but the dumbass skiers' prescribed meds were turning off the lights in my mind, one by one, and then suddenly I was gone.

16.

The next morning, by the time I had showered and packed a toiletry bag, Frank's limo was outside waiting for my ass.

I looked into the guest room and saw that my civilian son was dead to the world. Ella was still asleep on the couch under an afghan my mother had knitted. It had a huge red apple in the center and our family name at the top in green: GRANGER. My dead mother would have liked the fact that her afghan was keeping her great-granddaughter warm. I thought about how this perhaps might be the last time I would ever see Hank and Ella if that big Indian motherfucker were to keep his promise and scalp me. I knew I was still tough enough to win a fight against Fire Bear, but maybe I'd end up losing so much blood being half scalped that it might prove fatal, especially after my brain surgery—so I drank my family in for an extra few seconds.

In the limo Frank had coffee for me. He let me get in one smoke with the window down before we got on the highway. When I flicked the butt and rolled up the window, he patted my thigh and said, "You have the knife?"

I pulled it out of my camouflage jacket and showed it to

him. He looked it over and then said I was doing the right thing.

I asked if Frank was sure Fire Bear wouldn't try to scalp me. He laughed and said he guaranteed no one was getting scalped, but he had never even met this tall crazy Indian motherfucker, so his promise rang hollow, as they say.

Since Frank wouldn't let me smoke on his jet, I sucked a few Marlboros down on the tarmac and then slapped the nicotine patch he gave me onto my bicep.

The pilots were ex-military, so I knew we were okay there, even though they were fucking squids, meaning navy. I busted their balls a little, and they talked shit against the army too, but it was all good, because we weren't touchy liberals who couldn't stand to have their balls busted for any reason at all. The military had made us mentally stronger than that. If you can't stand a little name-calling, you sure as hell aren't going to hold up under fire, and don't you forget it.

Because he's a spoiled billionaire, Frank has a fucking bed in his jet. Once we were in the air, he said he hadn't gotten much sleep since I last saw him—which meant he had been having sex with a thirty-year-old model nonstop, so don't go feeling too bad for him—and then he retired to his "private chamber."

I sipped my coffee and looked out at the clouds and laughed. Frank was getting old. Time was, he could grind a model mistress all night long and still have enough energy left over to be a real man in the morning. Now he needed to take naps when he was with his buddies, just so his ability to model-fuck would not decline.

I'd never want to date a woman forty years younger than me because I'm still in love with Jessica, but to each his own.

Maybe you are feeling bad for Frank's wife. If you met her even once, you wouldn't. That bitch has spent millions and millions of dollars on lady hats alone. She has a whole wing of their mansion dedicated to nothing but lady hats. She has done absolutely *nothing* for the past three decades except shop for lady hats. She could feed any country in Africa for a year just by selling her lady-hat collection. So it is what it is.

As we flew west, I palmed my father's and my lucky dog tags, which always make me feel calm when I'm traveling by air. I'd never fly without them. And I looked down at the vast land I had fought to defend from the threat of communism and little yellow bastards and felt a small amount of pride.

I saw farms and mountains and rivers and cities and clouds and communities, which all contained millions of unseen American lives—people like Hank and Ella and Sue and Big T and Timmy and Johnny, just trying to get through ninety or so years without fucking up too badly, maybe hoping for a few laughs along the way and the freedoms and liberties necessary to get the job done.

I've always hated the Dallas Cowgirls football team because they have won so many Super Bowls while my Eagles have never hoisted a Super Bowl trophy high in the air, so it was easy to see why the rest of the world hated America, even as they tried so desperately to break through our borders to become part of us. Everyone is jealous of a winner, and America is the biggest winner of all. Why were we all lucky enough to be born here, instead of some other shithole country? That was one of God's great mysteries, I guessed, and then thought I'd ask God directly if He let me the fuck into heaven, which wasn't likely, to say the least.

Twenty or so minutes before we landed, Frank emerged from his private room, poured himself a cup of coffee, and sat in the lounge chair across from me. He asked if I wanted him to buy me a suit, and I said that I preferred camouflage while my brain healed. "I've always been toughest in my army-issued clothing," I explained.

"You were a hard-ass banker for decades. You wore a suit and tie every day back then," Frank said. "Hell, you were the toughest man in a suit I ever met."

"That was before this," I said, and pointed to the scar on my head.

Frank nodded. He always wore a suit and tie—that was his uniform. Even if we went to the Phillies game in the middle of the summer he wore a suit, and I respected that. But he'd never traded bullets with gooks in the jungle, and the government had never cracked open his skull either.

I asked him if he still thought this Indian business was a good idea, and he said it was.

To protect the innocent, I'm not going to say exactly where we landed, but we caught a few amazing views of mountains on the way down, and then we were on another tarmac.

I ripped off the nicotine patch and sucked down a few Marlboros before we hopped into another limousine and drove off to a mountain lodge hotel of sorts that sat proudly on a few acres of prime American real estate.

Lots of animal heads hung on the walls, and the lobby fireplace was big enough to fit Shadrach, Meshach, and Abednego and then some, for those of you future readers who have actually read the Bible. Frank had booked us into a huge suite with a hot tub in the living room that had a glass ceiling over it so that we could look up at the stars. Which is exactly what we did, with Cuban cigars hanging out of our mouths, after we ate a big steak dinner made from cows that had lived less than ten miles away. I ate my steak under a pair of bull horns hung on the wall behind me. Classic Americana. It was a nice place, and I had to laugh at how far I had come from eating snakes and sleeping in fucking trees.

Damn right, America is a good place to live if you're hardworking and realistic about the world.

It is not gay to be naked and alone in a hot tub with your best man friend, provided that you are smoking cigars and no part of your body touches his at any point, and so we made sure to stay on opposite sides, getting in and out at different times so our white asses wouldn't accidentally bump together when they were all hot and slippery. The hotel had these thick bathrobes that were like wearing the best blanket you have ever encountered, and so we put those on and finished the cigars on the couch while Frank sipped some sort of Scotch that probably cost per glass more than you will net in six months.

Frank said that the next day was going to be a good one for me, and I said that there was a good chance the big Indian might try to scalp me after all, and I couldn't be held responsible for my actions if I had to defend myself.

Frank frowned and said, "Are you the same scared kid you were in the jungle fifty years ago?"

I told him I was never fucking scared, and that's when he said the point was that we had changed, which meant that Fire Bear had surely changed too.

Frank and I had changed for the better, but not all Vietnam veterans had. I thought about that fucking rapist, Brian, I had killed, and how Jessica's brother, Roger Dodger, had been killed in prison a year before Jessica lit herself on fire. Roger Dodger had gotten caught mugging women to keep up his drug habit, even though Jessica and I tried to help him right his ship many times. We made dozens of phone calls on his behalf, trying to get him job interviews. He mostly hadn't shown up for them, and when he did, he was always wasted, so I offered to pay for help with the drugs and drinking, but he only took that money and got high. Some people you just can't help, and they end up getting shanked in a jail drug deal gone bad. What a fucking waste. And all after surviving Vietnam too.

But Clayton Fire Bear was now a successful lawyer, I told myself over and over, and you don't become the head of a law firm by literally scalping white people in America. Metaphorically scalping all types of people is what *all* lawyers—red or yellow, black or white—do every day of the year, but that's another story.

I kept telling myself that Fire Bear was going to be cool about everything as I stretched out in the California king bed Frank made sure I had in my room.

People always say that old cliché about how you have to walk a day in another man's moccasins if you want to truly understand him, only no one ever says that about men who actually wear moccasins, meaning real American Indians. So

I tried to think about all that had happened from Fire Bear's point of view, wearing his moccasins, which were uncomfortable on my white feet, to say the least.

Then I started to think about Jessica again, and the name carved into her underwear drawer.

I had only slept for an hour by the time the clock said 5:00 a.m. I got the coffee going and then took a hot shower before I lined up my many pills and watched the sun come up over the distant mountains. I sipped coffee and smoked my first morning cigarette—Frank had been kind enough to book us a smoking suite, which still existed in this part of the country. He found me a few minutes later. He was showered and in his suit uniform and smiling over a cup of coffee himself.

We chowed down on breakfast at the hotel, and everyone there kept thanking me for my service, being that I was in my camouflage and we were in a part of the country where they really know how to treat veterans. I thought of how proud my father was when I took him back to Normandy, and it made me miss the old man something fierce. But I just nodded and smiled at the people who said nice words to me, because there isn't really a good response to someone thanking you for your service.

"You ready for this?" Frank said as we finished our bison sausage and eggs.

I told him that I had remembered the knife, if that was what he was worried about.

But it turns out he was worried about my emotional state, which was kind of him, so I told him he didn't need to get his panties in a twist for me. That made him laugh in a good way, and then reach over to swat me on the shoulder twice, the way guys do with their true buddies.

And then we were in another limo, headed into a small city that I will not name here, but there was snow everywhere, and the white mountains in the distance were lit so bright from the sun, it hurt your eyes to look.

Next there were tons of people clogging the sidewalks, walking in boots and heavy coats and even ski goggles, which made me think of my neurologist surgeon, asshole that he was.

The limo stopped in front of a modern-looking building with an all-mirrored-glass front that looked like something you might see in New York City. You could tell that whoever owned the building had class and big-time money, so I had mixed emotions when I saw Fire Bear's real last name written out in big letters.

I was glad that a fellow Vietnam veteran had overcome hardship and made something so obviously impressive of himself, but I knew that you never want to fuck with a powerful lawyer who can break your legal kneecaps in a court of law without even hardly trying. If I were going to lawyer up against a man who owned a big-time business like this, I would need more money than I currently had, which was a lot, but nothing compared to men like Frank. I had successful big-boy money, but Frank's made billions. And from the look of this building, it seemed like Fire Bear was somewhere in between.

And here I was, walking onto his home field with a knife I stole from him a lifetime ago. I was like a killer strolling into the police station fifty years after committing the crime, holding up the murder weapon the cops had spent their entire careers searching for.

Frank saw the doubt on my face. "Do you think I would let you do this if there were any possibility whatsoever that it could go sour?" he said.

I realized this meant that Frank had probably contacted Fire Bear—they might have e-mailed or spoken on the phone. The outcome might be rigged from the start, but I still had to walk through the door and face a soldier I had wronged when I was a young man.

You don't have to be a genius to realize that Fire Bear represented much more than our little story—he was symbolic of every fucked-up thing I had ever done in Vietnam, which was a long list, to say the least.

So I smoked a cigarette out there on the sidewalk, trying to find the courage, as Frank put his arm around me and told me everything was going to be okay. He kept saying I should trust him and that he had my best interests at heart and that I needed to do this because most Vietnam vets never get to right a single one of their wrongs. Frank kept saying over and over that I was doing this for every dumb young American combat veteran who has ever made mistakes, which was all of us, including Fire Bear.

It took me two more cigarettes to get up the courage. By then, I was so fucking cold from standing out there on the sidewalk that I just wanted to get warm. We went inside, and Frank checked in with the woman behind the desk in the lobby, saying that we were there to meet the big boss, Fire Bear himself. She told us to take a seat on these couches covered in real spotted cowhides.

Ten minutes later she told us to follow her, so we did that too, taking an elevator ride up to the top floor and then walking down a long hall with pictures of tepees and feather headdresses, along with all the other Indian-related shit that hung on the walls.

When we got to Fire Bear's office, there were two cigar-store Indians flanking the door. That made me want to take a picture—Hank always insisted that those were racist, yet Fire Bear had chosen them to guard his office.

My nemesis was seated behind his desk, his back turned. He was looking out his window, which had a million-dollar view of the distant mountains. The good-looking lady who had escorted us to Fire Bear's office said, "Mr. Fire Bear, David Granger is here to see you."

Fire Bear didn't respond.

I looked at Frank. He nodded, meaning I was to go in alone. So I did.

I heard the door close behind me, and my heart started to pound.

As I approached, Fire Bear said "Sit," so I sat in one of two red leather chairs facing his desk. He did not turn around, nor did he speak for what seemed like an eternity, so I told him I had his father's knife and wanted to return it to him. He didn't say anything in response.

He just kept staring out the window, his back turned.

Fire Bear had aged just like the rest of us. There was a lot of silver in his hair now, and his broad shoulders were slumped, suggesting that time had ground him down a bit too. I got to feeling guilty and ashamed, sitting there in his office, thinking about what I had done to him almost fifty years ago in Vietnam.

So I started rambling, saying I had orders back in the jungle, I was just a child, and everyone who had been engaged in combat for so many days was legally insane. I heard an urgency in my voice as I tried to defend myself. I could talk to Fire Bear about these things, I realized, because he was a veteran; he had been there.

Finally, I just said I was sorry. I put the knife on his desk. I told him it was his, and I didn't want anything for it; I just wanted to give it back.

Then he asked if I had found his name carved into Jessica's underwear drawer, which made me shiver. His voice was nothing like I remembered it. The hot anger was no longer there, which was a relief, to say the least.

I wanted to kill him for presumably breaking into my home all those years ago, but I also wanted to know what the fuck had happened, and why Jessica never told me about any of it.

When I didn't say anything, Fire Bear spilled it all without turning around to face me. His voice was so deep and it seemed to scrape the inside of his throat on the way out.

A few years after his discharge from Fort Riley, he had driven his old pickup truck across the entire country, just to visit our home in New Jersey and make good on his promise to scalp me. He waited until he thought maybe I had forgotten all about him, using that line about how revenge is a dish best served cold. He entered my home on a weekday afternoon, when he figured I'd be at work, because he wanted to use the knife I had stolen to do the scalping. He had to find it first, and then he would kill me. Part one would be much easier if he could search my home when I wasn't there. What he didn't know is that I used to carry his knife on me when I went to work, so he searched my house but couldn't find shit.

With a backup knife he had brought with him, Fire Bear carved his name in Jessica's underwear drawer, hoping she would find it and ask me what it meant, which would force me to either lie or explain the unimaginable shit I did in Vietnam. He also wanted to send me a clear death threat. But as he was finishing that carving, he heard Hank start crying in the other room. Immediately, he knew that the best revenge was to kill my son.

Fire Bear stood over the crib with the knife in his hand, watching tiny, vulnerable Hank wail. He tried and tried to get up the stones to take revenge on the white man who had humiliated and abused him in the jungle before stealing a family heirloom. *Do it! Do it! Do it!* he told himself.

Obviously, Fire Bear never went through with his plan to kill Hank. But the pause he threw into the story at this point was terrible anyway, especially since he hadn't moved at all. My nemesis sat like a statue, facing the window, the whole time he talked.

Finally, Fire Bear said, he heard a woman's voice. When he turned around, he saw Jessica standing in the hallway. She had been in her art studio when he first entered our home. He still had the knife in his hand, so it was pretty clear what he had come to do.

But then Jessica asked him why he was crying. That shocked Fire Bear because he didn't realize he *was*. So he put a hand to his face, and found out that he was indeed crying, and hard.

That's when he sort of lost it, falling to his knees, realizing that he was about to kill an innocent child. The knife fell out of his hand, and the next thing he knew, my wife had her arms around him and she was trying to comfort him, which made him cry even harder, because he'd been just about to stab her baby, and here she was trying to make *him* feel better.

But Jessica understood what it was like to be angry and depressed and insane from time to time. If he had run up against any other woman, he might be in jail right now. Most women would have called the cops right then and there. But it turns out that Jessica even allowed Fire Bear to hold Hank, and she explained what I had done for them both—that Hank wasn't even my flesh and blood, but I had pretended to be his father after Brian raped her. Fire Bear said he couldn't stop crying the whole time, he just sobbed and sobbed, because he felt so bad about what he had come to do and everything his government had forced him to do in the jungle. So Jessica tried to level him out, making him coffee and lunch and then even showing him a few of her paintings in the garage.

I couldn't believe what I was hearing, and yet it all made so much sense.

He talked about how her art made him feel, saying it was like she understood what was going on in his mind and heart. Jessica kept showing him more and more images, trying to get him to stop crying, and he said right there in the garage studio he reached out and hugged her and apologized for breaking into her home and trying to kill her baby and also for many other wicked things that he had done in Vietnam too.

She kept saying she forgave him, and every time she said it, he'd sob even harder until he knew he had to leave because I would surely be home from work soon, and he didn't think I would forgive him so easily.

He told Jessica that he forgave me, her husband, and that he would never return. The knife was now a gift that he had given our family. He would never come looking for it again.

Then he left.

There was a long silence here. It might have lasted twenty minutes. As you might imagine, neither of us knew what to say. And I was trying to decide whether I could possibly believe this story. As I stared at the back of Fire Bear's head, I realized he was making himself vulnerable by turning his back to me. Vietnam veterans don't like to have anyone behind them, out of sight, let alone a potential enemy. Fire Bear was no longer my nemesis. That's when I decided to trust him.

Finally I said, "She never told me any of this."

"I understand that your wife is no longer with us?" he said, letting me know that Frank had clued him in a bit.

So I told him what had happened to Jessica, how she not only killed herself when Hank was still just a boy but burned all her paintings, and how Hank was now an art dealer, and his biggest regret in life was never seeing a single one of his own mother's artworks. I was rambling.

Eventually I fell quiet. After another long silence, Fire Bear spun his chair around and faced me. There were tears running down his wrinkled face. His once-sharp jawline now sagged, just like mine. He was dressed in a sharp suit that looked exactly like one of Frank's, and his hair was cut like a white man's. No braids or feathers or anything like that.

His eyes fell for a second to the knife on his desk, which he hadn't seen since he was in Vietnam back in sixty-seven. Then he said he was very sorry for my loss and asked if Frank and I would join him at his house for dinner that evening so that we could break bread and heal old wounds. After all he had shared with me, I agreed to the invitation immediately.

Then he asked if I would please bring his father's knife to dinner, because he wanted his son to see it.

I told him that the knife was his—that I had come all this way to return it.

He nodded once and said he had given me the knife when Jessica was so kind to him, but would I please bring it to dinner that evening, so his son might at least see it.

I agreed, thinking I would give it to his son when I met him, because that was the right thing to do. We stood and shook hands over his desk.

It was funny—in my memory, for decades, I'd thought of Fire Bear towering over me, but he was only an inch taller than yours truly, so just about six feet tall.

I didn't know what else to say, so I picked up the knife and said I would bring it that evening. He said his secretary would provide directions to his home and show us out, which she did.

In the limo I told Frank everything that I had learned. Frank agreed that giving the knife to Fire Bear's son was the noble thing to do. We immediately went in search of a gay florist so that we could bring Fire Bear's wife a proper flower arrangement, and we also shopped for high-end wine and Scotch.

Time passed strangely that day, both quickly and slowly. The part of me that just wanted to give the knife to Fire Bear's son and then go home felt like the day went on forever. But another part of me was afraid of facing Fire Bear's family, wondering if they knew how cruel I had been to him during the war, and that part felt like time was flying by.

Soon enough we were back in the limousine, headed to Fire Bear's place, which was outside the city, closer to the mountains. His house was more like a log-cabin castle that sat upon a few hundred acres.

When Frank and I went inside, we were surprised to find Fire Bear's entire family there—his wife, three daughters, son, their spouses, and ten or so grandchildren, ages infant to maybe seventeen. I don't remember all of the names, and I wouldn't list them here now anyway. But we were introduced all around, and Fire Bear—who wore jeans, cowboy boots, and a flannel shirt now—kept saying I was his "friend" from the Vietnam War. That's when I realized that he had never told the truth about me to his family—or the truth about himself.

All the kissing and handshaking made me feel so welcome, I was embarrassed. None of them asked why I was in full camouflage, either, although I did show off my scar, and we talked about my surgery at length.

Scanning Fire Bear's children and grandchildren, I saw that he was lucky—there were no Agent Orange birth defects. He'd been exposed at least as much as I had. And he hadn't gotten the cancer, either. Maybe God was trying to even things out a bit, being that he was born Indian, and already had enough hardship to manage.

Dinner was delicious. We all sat around a twenty-foot-long table that Fire Bear and his son had made by hand, and ate steaks cut from cows that Fire Bear's family had raised and slaughtered themselves. All of it was organic and grass-fed, and I wished Hank could have been there, because there was no way in hell he would have had the balls to tell a real live American Indian that eating the cows he'd raised himself was not heart-healthy.

Frank carried the conversation, asking them all what they did for a living and how they liked living in the area and all of those sorts of questions. Our wine and Scotch and flowers were a big hit, and it was nice to be around Fire Bear's family, all of whom seemed to be good Americans.

After some apple pie, which Fire Bear had to explain was a joke that his family had come up with, serving apple pie to the white guests—not a very funny joke, unfortunately—Fire Bear asked if his son could see the knife I stole decades ago, only he didn't say I stole it.

I immediately produced the knife and handed it to his son, who was about Hank's age, maybe a few years younger, but already had three sons of his own.

Fire Bear's son looked over the knife and announced that he would like to have it. Before I could tell him that it was already his, he asked if he might trade for the knife. A hush fell over the room. It began to feel like everyone was about to sing happy birthday to someone, or maybe like the moment you let your grandchildren see all the presents under the tree on Christmas morning. I could tell that these Indians had a surprise for me, but at first I had no idea what it could be.

"Would you consider trading me for this knife?" Fire Bear's son said again, only now he was smiling ear to ear, showing off his remarkably white teeth.

It was obvious that we were doing a bit of theater here, and I had been to enough musicals to know when the happy ending was about to occur. The audience can always feel these things, and I was obviously the audience for this little almost-all-Indian play—*almost*, because I now understood that Frank was performing too, definitely in cahoots with these remarkably nice people.

Suddenly I couldn't speak. I was hoping that I knew what Fire Bear's son was going to offer me, yet I didn't want to dare dream it was possible. Frank put his arm around me and squeezed me hard, which is when I realized that a big tear was rolling down my face. I wiped it away, and then Fire Bear's son stood and said, "Let's go to the den." Almost two dozen Indians stood in unison, and we all walked through a few rooms to the other end of the gigantic log-cabin mansion.

There it was, hanging on the wall over the fireplace.

It was me in full camouflage and naked baby Hank, his umbilical cord not yet cut but circling us to form a protective bubble of sorts, keeping the napalm and tigers and little yellow men and Agent Orange at bay.

I looked at Fire Bear and said, "How?" which Hank probably would suggest was an insensitive thing to say to an Indian, but I didn't mean it that way. I just wanted to know how one of

Jessica's paintings had survived. Plus, I couldn't get any other words out. I was shaking like an FNG in a firefight.

Fire Bear told me that my wife had given him the painting when he "visited" my home after the war. They had wrapped it in old sheets and trash bags to protect it as it rode in the back of his pickup across the country, and he'd kept it because Jessica's kindness on that day was the spark he needed to turn his life around. And what I did for Hank, saving him, was enough for Fire Bear to let go of his own anger. Whenever he got to feeling angry about what the US government made him do in the Vietnam War, he would simply look at Jessica's painting, think about all that was associated with it, and that would help.

Fire Bear's son carefully took *The Reason You're Alive* off the wall, and this is when I noticed that they had prepared a special box to protect the painting as it traveled back to the Philadelphia area with us. Six or seven of them helped to wrap Jessica's masterpiece and get it all padded and protected in the box, and then Fire Bear's son said, "So do we have a deal?"

I nodded, and we shook hands. Fire Bear said, "I understand your son will appreciate having this painting?"

I looked over at Frank. He just shrugged, even though I realized he had set this all up.

Fire Bear put his big, weathered hand on my camouflaged shoulder. "Let him know I held him when he was a baby, and that his mother saved my life, okay?"

I nodded, because I couldn't speak. That morning I'd been worried I might be scalped, and here I was among the warmest people I will probably ever meet, no matter how long I live. I hugged every single one of Fire Bear's family members, and even though I couldn't make my mouth work, they seemed to understand that I was grateful as could be.

Just before I left, Fire Bear's son—who is also a lawyer, by the way—shook my hand and thanked me for returning the property of his ancestors.

And then Frank and I were in the limousine with the painting, which just barely fit into the trunk, and driving back to the hotel. I wanted to open up the box there and look at Jessica's art, worried that this all had been a dream, but Frank said we better not—we didn't have anyone around to help us get it packed up the right way so it wouldn't be damaged on the flight home.

And so I skipped the hot tub and went to sleep right away, hoping the hours would pass by fast. I wanted to give my art-loving son the very painting he'd waited his whole life to see.

17.

On the flight home, Frank went into his private room again. I had a lot of time to think about all that had happened during my time as an American.

Hank would say that I was lucky to be born white and to have powerful and influential friends like Frank, also white. But what Hank didn't understand is that a lot of people born white in America don't amount to shit, nor do they ever take rides on private jets.

I have often wondered how the fuck I made as much money as I did, coming out of a mostly blue-collar neighborhood. No doubt my skin color made it easier for me, especially in the seventies and eighties, but there seemed to be more to it than that.

Also, I don't consider the post-Vietnam horror show playing endlessly between my ears for damn near fifty years a lucky thing, nor Jessica's burning herself to death.

It was easy to point to Fire Bear and say that if he could make it in America, any race or color could. Any moron with a library card understands that the US government fucked the Indians worse than any other race—Fire Bear no doubt had to be the Jackie Robinson of Indian lawyers to overcome all the obstacles thrown his way as he fought to get his in the land of the free.

Fire Bear might have been unlucky being born Indian during a time when the white man ruled, but he was definitely lucky to have met up with Jessica when he broke into our home. I would have fucking killed him. And we were both lucky that Death had remained our mutual friend in Vietnam, allowing us to carry on when so many other lives were snuffed out.

It was easy for Hank to scream and yell about white privilege: no one had ever tried to take anything away from him. He thought his so-called white privilege came to him like his DNA.

Fire Bear and his entire family knew the game. Frank knew it too. Big T and his brothers understood. So did Timmy and Johnny. Even Sue had a clue. And I thought about how I was lucky enough to know all of them. Maybe it didn't matter if my son was a bleeding-heart liberal moron, just as long as there were people like me and my friends to keep him in check.

When Frank emerged from his private chamber, maybe twenty minutes before we landed in the City of Brotherly Love, I didn't launch into a long bullshit speech proclaiming my thanks. Instead, I reached over and squeezed his shoulder. I looked him in the eye.

He nodded.

I nodded back.

We transferred the painting into a limousine waiting on the tarmac for us, and then we drove to Hank's house.

As we turned the corner of Hank's block and pulled up to

his home, I asked Frank if my son had any idea about what we had in the trunk. Frank said Hank was clueless, as always. Frank also told me to enjoy what was about to happen.

"You're not coming in?" I asked.

"It's family business," he said.

I told Frank that he was part of my family, and he smiled and told me that he had some "mentoring" to do in the city, which was his way of saying man up and do the right thing, because these types of life-altering father-son bonding opportunities don't pop up every fucking day.

He was right. I nodded and told him to enjoy his mentoring. But then I couldn't resist adding, "You're a good man," breaking our code.

He let it slide by punching my shoulder and saying, "Go."

So I did.

Frank's driver helped me carry the painting up to Hank's door. When he opened up, my son said, "What is that?"

I told him it was fucking cold outside, so let us in and I would explain all.

Femke was there, he said, and I said that what I had couldn't wait, regardless of whether his house was infested with the Dutch or not.

Once the driver and I got the painting into Hank's living room, the driver tipped his little black hat and made his exit. Femke and Ella walked in from the kitchen, and my granddaughter announced that they were making rainbow sprinkle cookies. She asked if I would like to try one, so I said sure.

The cookie was warm and colorful, but I could tell my presence was making Femke uncomfortable. I said I had a present for Hank, but I didn't want to make too big of a deal about this, so we would just open it and agree that there would be no hugging or crying.

Hank got this really strange look in his eyes. I knew that he knew what was in the box, because he started peeling off the tape without even asking if he could. Ella started clapping and cheering her father on, but Femke had her hand over her mouth, which clued me in, letting me know that she knew what was in the box too. Say what you want about the Dutch, but they are not stupid.

By the time Hank had got the large painting free and started demummifying it, he was shaking violently. When he saw my young face and his umbilical cord and Jessica's signature in orange paint at the bottom corner, he started to sob. It scared the hell out of Ella, who just hugged his leg and wouldn't let go. Femke was crying too on the other side of the room. I decided to go have a cigarette in the backyard. I had been through enough emotions in the last few days to last seven lifetimes.

I could hear kids playing basketball a few houses down, yelling and screaming and trying to break the backboard with all the brick shots they were throwing at it. I lit up and watched the smoke leave my mouth and fly up to the sky. By the time Hank came outside with red eyes and started asking questions, I'd smoked three and a half.

I gave Hank a civilian version of all I have explained here, even finally admitting that I wasn't his real father, and therefore not Ella's real grandfather either, and that I had kept everything from him in the past because I was trying to protect him from the truth. I didn't tell him that Brian had raped his mother, or that, consequently, I had killed his biological father. Instead, I went with the widely believed story that Brian had simply overdosed on drugs, and told Hank that I'd stepped up to the plate because he needed a father.

That was when he asked me about the title of the painting, which was apparently written on the back of the frame:

THE REASON YOU'RE ALIVE

I confirmed it was the original title. I couldn't think up a good lie to cover for Jessica, so I just endured the awkward silence as Hank puzzled out the meaning.

Finally, Hank asked if his mother was going to abort him. Had I had talked her out of that plan?

For various reasons, abortions weren't exactly easy to get back then, I told him.

Then finally Hank figured it out on his own. He looked me in the eye and—with a wounded expression that seemed to conjure little vulnerable elementary-school Hank—he said, "She was going to kill herself with me inside her."

It wasn't a question, so I didn't answer it. Instead, I lit up two cigarettes, and we smoked in silence.

Halfway through the smoke, Hank said, "Mom was an even better painter than you made her out to be." Then he started up with his art-world bullshit talk, even asking if the Fire Bears had hung Jessica's painting over the fireplace—apparently that was a big no-no, and meant that Hank would have to get our painting professionally cleaned. I understood he was talking about all of this shit so he didn't have to talk about the harder stuff. I let it slide. Civilians exhale bullshit the way veterans exhale air. And I had learned that long ago.

Femke stuck her head out and said that dinner was ready, so I told Hank I should leave, but he said he wanted me to stay, and so did the rest of his family. I was doubtful about that, but then Hank asked Femke if she wanted me to stay for dinner, which is when she came outside and kissed me on the cheek. I thought for sure she was playing Judas until she said, "You did a good thing today and I won't forget it."

That was the nicest sentence I ever heard come out of the Dutch woman's mouth, and it made me want to forget about her fucking a weatherman, even though I never could.

I had to laugh when Femke served me nothing but an entire plate of kale, sautéed radishes, and beets, just like you knew she would. And there wasn't even salad dressing, just half a lemon squeezed over my plate, though at least I was offered a pinch of sea salt that the rest of my family could not have, because it wasn't heart-healthy.

And I thought right then and there that white privilege did not cover food these days. The Indians and blacks and genetically Vietnamese people I had broken bread with ate so much better than my family. But I decided to keep my mouth shut and listen to Ella go on and on about the play her school was performing. Somewhere in there Femke asked if I would like a ticket, which meant she was trying hard to win me over. I knew my son didn't have the balls to kick the Dutch out forever. I realized that I had better get political and so I said I would like a ticket, which made Femke smile.

While Femke was tucking in Ella, no doubt combing her

hair like I did in Femke's absence, Hank sat down on the sofa next to me and said he would always consider me his father, regardless of the fact that we weren't blood. I just nodded, thinking Hank was using too many words again, making everything awkward, but I appreciated the gesture.

We were admiring Jessica's painting. I could see what he meant about it being hung over a fireplace—in the light, you could see the smoke damage—but you couldn't really blame the Indians for that. Being that they used to live in tepees with a fire in the middle, you could easily see how they would make that mistake.

Sitting there on the couch with Hank, I had a strange thought, and for some reason I let it escape my mouth. I told Hank that I had chosen him when he had no one else in the world because he was a baby, and here he was choosing me, now that the US government had sliced out part of my brain after spraying me with Agent Orange.

"So in the end," Hank said, getting cocky, "you were saved by a liberal who voted for Obama. Is that what you're saying?"

It was just like my son to bring everything back to his dumb politics, but I liked the fact that he was busting my balls a little. Maybe there was hope for him after all.

18.

I had a big fight with Sue. She didn't want me to wear camouflage to her wedding but a monkey suit tuxedo instead. I told her I would wear my camouflage jacket and cargo pants and bucket hat just like every other day of the year, because tuxedos were for men weaker than me. Sue actually cried when I told her this, which caught me off guard. I had never seen her get so emotional before.

Big T entered the debate to work on a compromise. If it were up to him, he said, he would surely let me wear whatever the fuck I wanted, but weddings were for women, which is true, and so he wanted to give his woman whatever she wanted on her special day.

Big T had been spending more time with Hank, and had even gotten him to attend some springtime Phillies games with us, which I appreciated. I would always love Hank more than Teddy, but when it came to watching sports, truth be known, I enjoyed hanging out with Big T much more than I enjoyed hanging out with Hank.

Finally, I agreed to go to the tuxedo shop and see the monkey suit Big T had picked out for me. When the salesperson hung up my tuxedo on the display rack, I immediately noticed that while the pants and jacket were black, the tie and vest were camouflage. I looked at Big T, and he said, "I got you," so I tried on the tux and acquiesced, which made Sue cry again.

She was goddamn confusing during the buildup to her wedding, changing her mind about everything a million times. Big T kept calling her Bridezilla, but only when she wasn't around. Me, personally, I just couldn't wait for the wedding to be over so that Sue would start acting normal again and we could all go on with our lives.

Finally the day came, and I walked Sue down the aisle. She was beautiful, in a white dress with a long train behind her and Ella walking in front of us, holding flowers, along with one of Big T's nieces.

There was a woman preacher, which no doubt made Femke and Hank happy. They were both invited, even though I told Sue she didn't have to feel obligated. Timmy and Johnny were there too. Even Frank got an invite, although I told Sue and Big T to make sure that happened, because Frank always puts a shitload of cash into a wedding card, and I didn't want them to miss out on that.

I wondered about Sue's biological family back in Vietnam, especially since Hank had finally been in touch with his biological paternal family, saying that he at least wanted genetic information regarding diseases so that both Ella and he could watch for warning signs throughout life. I was okay with that, especially since Femke was playing nice now, and it felt like we were all solid otherwise.

At the reception, to open things up, Sue and I danced to

Stevie Wonder's "Isn't She Lovely," no doubt so that Sue could impress her new family, being that Stevie Wonder is a black musical genius. He's also blind, and I have already told you about my fear of blind people, but I managed to control that long enough to get through the many dance practices Sue put me through, which were physically more demanding than training with Gay Timmy. But I did my best on the big night and—to be fair—Sue did most of the spinning around and showboating while I sort of stayed in one spot, just guiding her, or so it appeared to the untrained eye.

And when everyone was clapping at the end of our dance, she whispered into my ear—which I had cleaned free of hair using the trimmer Hank gave me—and said she loved me. I told her that her father, Alan, would be damn proud of her, and then she was off with Big T, grooving with the young people.

Timmy and Johnny were dancing with Ella and Femke and Hank, and a lot of Teddy's friends were trying to get the white people out of their seats, and eventually everyone but me was on the dance floor, having so much fun.

I watched for a bit, and then I went outside for a smoke. I could still hear the music, but it was a lot quieter.

With all that had happened, I was already exhausted on account of the fucking brain meds. To be truthful, I had also gotten to missing Jessica again. I missed her every day of my life, but there was something about attending a wedding with everyone I loved except her—seeing two young people like Sue and Big T starting off a marriage in that good hopeful beginning place, all while mine had ended so fucking tragically more than thirty years ago. I didn't want to make the day about me, because it wasn't, but I also couldn't help the way I was feeling. So I just lit up and started puffing.

Jessica is what they call a conundrum. If Roger Dodger and I hadn't fought in the Vietnam War, Jessica and I would have never met. And yet I'm pretty sure that our being in the war is exactly what ended my marriage and Jessica's life early.

My wife was a sensitive person, too in tune with the world. If most people receive life's radio frequency at volume four, she received it at volume one hundred million. So while you might read this here report and ponder it for a few hours before going on with your trivial civilian lives, forgetting—just like everyone else—what Vietnam veterans went through during and after the war, Jessica internalized everything, both metaphorically and literally, when you think about the fucking rape and Hank growing in her belly, and so she would never ever stop thinking about all this shit for one single second for the rest of her life. She simply was unable. She never fully recovered from the early blows life dealt her, and I don't think I had the tools to help her the way she needed to be helped. I saved her ass when she was a pregnant teenager, and I gave her unlimited art supplies and a studio to paint in, but she obviously needed more than that.

Even before the war, I was a hardheaded asshole. My mother always used to say so. I was born set in my ways, and I'm not sure my ways were good for Jessica in the long run. So maybe her killing herself doesn't have anything to do with the Vietnam War at all. But then I go back to thinking about why she went to that drug house and how far gone her brother was and how that affected her at a young age, which was compounded by all of my crazy baggage.

Jessica developed all sorts of tricks for dealing with me. The first time we slept in a bed together, I had the fucking nightmares like always and started screaming in my sleep. I had told her never to wake me up under any circumstance whatsoever, but she didn't listen, so the next thing I remember, she's on the floor and I'm holding a knife to her throat. I regained consciousness and came to my senses just in time to refrain from opening up her jugular. Not a great way to start off a romance, to say the least. But Jessica learned and adapted.

She didn't wake me up from then on, but sang lullabies to me whenever I started to scream, and whispered through the darkness that she was with me and everything was okay. Sometimes this stopped my screaming completely. Other times I simply woke up, which was just as good. It took time to implant this trigger in my brain, meaning I would subconsciously associate her voice with safety. It became a switch to turn off the horror movie in my mind. Some nights she would sing and whisper for hours before I stopped screaming, and you can imagine what that did to her own circadian rhythms or whatever the fuck you call them.

Roger Dodger used to drain her too, coming around the house when he knew I was at work, distracting her from Hank and her paintings, trying to steal shit from our home to sell. He once stole all our silverware and the TV set when Jessica was in her studio, and yet she used to make him coffee and listen to him rant about the war and the government and how America was a scam and his wild theories about Light People too. That shit takes a toll on a sensitive person. She was counseling two Vietnam veterans, and all while she was depressed herself.

But it wasn't all doom and gloom, especially when Hank was little and her painting was going well.

I got my first convertible in the mid-seventies—a mint 1969 Camaro, black with two thick white stripes on the hood. I bought it because I got a good deal, and my wife said driving around in the wind and sun would help with her depression. I remember Jessica and Hank absolutely loved feeling the air ripping through their hair and hand-surfing the world as it rushed by, and I was proud to have made enough money working at the bank and doing some other side investments to buy the car that they wanted.

The first trip we took in the Camaro was to a rented house in the Poconos, on a lake. It was summer, so I took off my shirt and drove the whole way like that, soaking up the rays, feeling free as could be, back before everyone was so goddamn worried about skin cancer. I might have even sipped from a can of Budweiser as I drove. And I remember looking over at Jessica, who was still only in her early twenties. She had her hair wrapped up in a silk scarf, and she had on these big oversize purple sunglasses, and she had even put on some lipstick, which was rare for her.

I felt so happy that I leaned over and kissed her right on the lips, which made her laugh. Then I looked into the rearview mirror and saw little Hank holding his hands up in the air and smiling at clouds, and I thought I was the luckiest man in the world. I had survived the little yellow bastards in Vietnam, and now I had a beautiful family in the land of the free and a promising career at the bank.

My father and mother were following behind us, and they

were still in good health at the time, being that they were just in their fifties, which is almost twenty years younger than I am now. And I remember holding up my hand in the air, beeping the horn and waving at my father. I could see him smiling in the rearview mirror, and he beeped back and then lifted his own worn, battle-tested hand up outside his window. I was taking all of us to the Poconos to celebrate my mother's birthday, I think. Yeah, that was it.

And I also remember swimming in the lake with my family and smoking with my father, both of us sitting at a wooden picnic table shaded by giant oaks, ashing into a flowerpot filled with sand. And my mother working the charcoal grill, cooking up the hot dogs and hamburgers, and Jessica in a bikini, looking like a top model herself as she used sticks to draw pictures in the sand with Hank.

Sitting right there on the picnic table by the lake, my father put his arm around me and said I was really doing okay, meaning he was proud of his only son who had made something of himself after returning from war, and I nodded back, because all I ever wanted in life was my hard-ass Nazi-killing father's approval, and I felt I had it on that warm good afternoon in the Poconos.

And later that night in the cottage I had rented, Jessica opened all the windows so that you could hear a billion fucking crickets chirping and the night birds singing their hunting songs, and you could even hear the glow of the full moon spilling over everything like ghostly milk. It must have been one of those rare nights when Jessica wasn't feeling depressed and I wasn't too fucking stressed from work, because we made love right there in the Poconos bed as my mother and father and Hank slept in rooms below us.

And when I was inside Jessica and kissing her neck, I suddenly felt a great sadness, because somehow I knew life would never ever get any better than that moment right then and there, which would be gone for good by the morning.

It never did either.

I was fucking right about that.

But I never stopped missing Jessica, the only woman for me, which is what made attending weddings hard.

Back outside Sue and Big T's party, I felt a hand on my shoulder. By the rough manly grip, I knew it was Frank, who I hadn't spoken with yet that evening, because his bitch wife hates me, and—despite my warnings—Sue said we had to invite her too.

Frank said something about our dancing days being done, and I told him a lot of our days were done.

So he busted my balls a little, asking if I was finally buying the bullet, and I told him that his ugly ass wasn't getting rid of me that easily.

That's when Frank started telling me all about your organization—how you collect stories from veterans like myself. He said that I had a fascinating tale to tell, and that civilians could learn a lot from it. Then he swore up and down that no one would edit my words, twisting everything to fit some bullshit political agenda.

I was worried that some of what I had to say could get me into legal trouble, because you never know what might happen when the thieving hypocritical US government gets a bug up its ass, and I don't trust lawyers and the current judicial system one bit. Plus I didn't know who the fuck you were, and still don't really.

And that's when Frank told me that there was the option of making my story into a "time capsule" that would not be read by anyone until after I was dead. This way I could tell the truth without fear of repercussions, and that made me feel a little better about the idea, especially because I could change names to protect the innocent and no one could fact-check with me after I was dead, so no fucking civilian idiots hounding me with stupid moronic questions.

Frank said that if we didn't document all of what had happened to us, it would be lost forever, and how could future generations learn from the past if only morons and the lying government wrote the history books without any rational, thinking, intelligent, cerebral people getting a say in there too.

There was no arguing with that logic.

Despite the fact that I'm clearly no storyteller, I finally told Frank I would do my part, even though I'm not stupid and therefore realize that you are most definitely connected to the US government somehow, even if Frank thinks otherwise.

Every fucking thing is connected to the US government. Can't get free of that, but fuck it, I'm done being silently complicit when it comes to the lies about my war and the good men you sent to fight it.

I could tell Frank was proud of me because he squeezed my shoulder once more and complimented me on the camouflage bow tie and vest. It was nice to have a friend like Frank, who was always offering me opportunities for closure when it came to the Vietnam War. And I felt lucky.

But all this is moot anyway, on account of the "time capsule" aspect, meaning no one sees any of this shit until I die.

Let me tell you something. Not gonna happen, because I'm gonna live forever.

So all of you fucking imbeciles who make up the so-called general public are *never* gonna see this report anyway.

Only the good die young, and I've lived nasty.

Live nasty, live forever.

Sweetheart, you can bet your pretty little ass on that.

ABOUT THE AUTHOR

MATTHEW QUICK is the *New York Times* bestselling author of several novels, including *The Silver Linings Playbook*, which was made into an Oscar-winning film; *The Good Luck of Right Now*; and *Love May Fail*. His work has been translated into more than thirty languages and has received a PEN/Hemingway Award Honorable Mention, among other accolades. He lives with his wife on North Carolina's Outer Banks.